ON THE WAY
TO PARADISE

Oct 30. 2013

ON THE WAY
TO PARADISE

A Stop Over In Perdition

James H. Greene

To order additional copies of this book, contact:
Xlibris Corporation
1-888-795-4274
www.Xlibris.com
Orders@Xlibris.com
27660

CONTENTS

Preface iii

Introduction v

Judas's Dilemma: Obstacles Blocking His Hearing 1

Before Time, Before Creation: The Teacher's Review of
    Being Dead 5

The Journey Begins: The Point of No Return—
    The Night of the First Day in Hades 10

The Fork in the Road: Etchers and Adheres 17

Tartarus 43

Adheres in Abraham's Bosom 48

Amadden 59

Etchers's Dilemma 87

Dawn of the First Day in Hades 104

Night of the Second Day 130

The Messiah's Entrance into Paradise 152

Salvation Comes to Paradise: Night to Dawn of the Third Day 164

Endnotes 181

Professor Greene continues his story focusing on Calvary and the four intertwined lives that through destiny met and died. As we follow the characters even though some are fictitious, we will begin to reflect on the life style that we have chosen, and determine what legacy we will have eternally.

Through this unique storytelling of the Gospel Message the readers, truly intrigued, will be able to identify themselves in its pages and embrace the Christ of Calvary.

God bless you Professor Greene for providing such a wonderful work of literary art.

In the service of the King,
Garry D. Zeigler
Pastor
Spirit Food Christian Center
Woodland Hills, CA

This book is dedicated to my mother, Jane Ogaro

Preface

This story is a continuation of the one previously written. The conversation in the previous episode is one that may be deemed fiction for want of a better explanation. However, knowing with whom we are dealing makes it unlikely to be anything but truth. "But Jesus looked at them and said to them, 'With men, this is impossible, but with God all things are possible.'"[1] God's love for us caused him to send his only begotten son into this world to live and feel as we do so that he could understand the depth of the problem of sin. Thus, he came to take that sin away from all who believed in him and confessed himself as the Christ, the only begotten son of God.

The first stage of this endeavor was played out on Calvary on a bleak, dreary day of darkness as the forces of good and evil faced off in the battle of all battles. What was at stake? The eternity of mankind. Some of the characters involved are fictitious; however, it is important to note that the names used for the thieves who died on the cross that day with Christ are symbolic.

"Etchers" is defined as someone who designs; to wit he designed not to follow his associate's lead and ask forgiveness from Christ. Instead, he followed the lifestyle that he had carved out, leading to his predictable end. He designed his end and did not try to change it. "Adheres" is defined as one who sticks fast or together. He chose to stick with Christ and, thus, embraced the opportunity to be forgiven and remembered. Christ forgave him at the end of his life as he knew, and he chose to change and cling to the man he recognized as the only one who could help him.

On that fateful day at Calvary, four men whose lives intertwined met and died. Their destination was prescribed by their actions while yet alive. Two of these men were destined for their permanent resting place: Hades. One of the other two was also headed for this place—for three days and nights—but then rendezvoused with the fourth man who was on his way to Abraham's bosom: paradise. The four initially traveled the same path but eventually separated for their earthly decisions.

Four men inextricably tied together for eternity. The first was Judas Iscariot, formerly a disciple of the one called teacher, now on his way to perdition or Hades. The other two were thieves, who died on both sides of the Messiah at Calvary Hill. One of the thieves, Etchers, joined the mockers to curse the Messiah. He and the crowd cursed the Messiah and dared him to come down from the cross in his might. The other thief, Adheres, was convicted of crimes against the state and humanity and sentenced to death like Etchers. Adheres understood and acknowledged the Messiah for who he was and pleaded with him, "Remember me when you come into your kingdom." The Messiah granted his desire. "Assuredly, I say to you, today you will be with me in paradise."

The fourth person was sentenced to death for the sins of all mankind. Calvary, a parched and windswept place outside Jerusalem, will forever mark the turning point in the history of mankind. It was the place from which the Messiah began the journey that would culminate in his triumphant reentry into this world, as the king and lord to some, and judge and jury to others.

Introduction

Death rejoiced at the thought that he had pulled off a coup on all eternity. He had witnessed the so-called Messiah accused, abused, and placed on a Roman cross. There was no way down from that tree except through him, and Death had no intention of releasing this Savior.

"The Creator will have to find another Messiah because this one is mine," he mused.

The demons and Satan too were ecstatic as they prematurely celebrated the seeming victory over the Creator, God, the omnipresent, omniscient one.

"Anytime now this Messiah would die, and Death would reign supreme over mankind for all eternity. Even Satan would have to contend with me when I pull this off!"

As Death reveled in his victory, something nagged inextricably at his unconscious. No matter how he tried, it stayed beyond his reach.

"Ah, he is crying out to the father," Death muttered to himself. "But he is not receiving a response! This is a wonderful day for me. Mankind is now mine, and even Satan will tremble at my name. If I can kill the Messiah, I can also kill Satan!"

These were the musings of Death as he viewed his handiwork . . . but the story had only just begun.

The silence was broken by the weeping of the women who were ever with the Messiah. Then the killer on the left made a statement that increased Death's confidence. He said, "If you are the Christ, save yourself and us."[2]

Still, the Messiah did nothing, and this bolstered Death's confidence that he had indeed won the battle. The Messiah was going down to Hades to be greeted by Satan and his minions who were already savoring the victory.

"Oh, this is an awesome day for me!"

Adheres rebuked Etchers, saying, "Do you not even fear God, seeing you are under the same condemnation? And we, indeed, justly, for we receive the due reward for our deeds; but this man has done nothing wrong."[3]

"He is quiet, but I know that he is not yet dead. Is he up to something?"

"This thing that is nagging me, I cannot shake it, but it will not make itself known."

"Oh well . . ."

The thief Adheres, who had just rebuked his colleague in crime, then spoke to the Messiah, asking him to do something that Death and the demons did not believe to be possible. He said to Jesus, "Lord, remember me when you come into your kingdom."[4]

Death, the demons, and Satan roared with laughter at the request. They envisioned all three of them in Hades together under the dominion of the forces of death and evil. Another man, Judas Iscariot, whom the devil had corrupted, was already on his way to Hades. Then the Messiah spoke, "Assuredly, I say to you, today you will be with me in paradise."[5]

Again the evil group laughed, with uncertainty this time. The alarm had gone off again, and Death could not determine what it meant.

"What does he mean . . . paradise?" Death wondered. "Is he talking about that other side where so many have been waiting . . . ? I remember a conversation that took place once, but . . . It evades me!"

Judas's Dilemma:
Obstacles Blocking His Hearing

"Judas? Judas? Judas!" a voice called out.

"Who is it?" Judas answered, "Where are you? Your voice sounds familiar. Is it you, Lord? No, it cannot be. I saw them take you, bind you, and lead you off. And I can guess what they have done to you. No, this must be my conscience. I took back the money in the first place, so I am not that awful.

"They tricked me, gave me only thirty pieces of silver, and I know that he is worth much more. Still, what I did was not right—to sell him because I was disappointed with him.

"I allowed evil to come into me through jealousy. I was such a fool!

I was the treasurer, handling much more than thirty pieces of silver! Ah! I was a fool!

"'What does it profit a man to gain the whole world and lose his soul?'[6]

"I made the biggest mistake of my life! And here I'm heading to a place that I did not consider. I wish that he would change his mind and forgive me, and deliver me from this predicament!

"I hurt him, I can see that, yet he may have mercy on me! I will go and appeal to him . . . but by now the high priest may have had him killed.

"For thirty pieces of silver, I betrayed the best friend that I ever had."

"Judas!" the voice called out again.

"It cannot be—he is dead! I have seen him work some awesome miracles but this . . . NO! It is my conscience.

"Knowing how the Pharisees hate him and the fact that the Passover is drawing near, they would have killed him already.

"But if he is killed immediately, then the deed is done, and the people would accept it. No, they will have killed him by now, so it cannot be him calling to me."

"Oh, Judas!" the voice went again.

"Hmm, maybe some wine will do the trick. I must clear my mind."

The voice came to him again and again. He tried to ignore it—without success. His conscience whipped him as the Jews whipped the Messiah. No wine or wandering could save him as the voice of the Messiah haunted him.

"Judas, you have spent enough time with me to know my voice, so answer me! You must shake off the evil that you have allowed to invade your mind and spirit! Listen to me, it is not too late for you to ask for and receive forgiveness for your wrongdoing!"

"Leave me alone!" Judas cried. "Am I to be tormented by this voice all the days of my life?"

As Judas wrestled with what he thought was his conscience, another voice chimed in, "You sold him for merely thirty pieces of silver, that is what and that is why."

"Oh, conscience, you are cruel! Leave me alone! I am sorry!"

"Yes, you are, but that is not enough!"

"I do not feel bad enough?" Judas asked.

"When you reach that point," the "conscience" advised, "then I will tell you what to do."

"Judas, do not listen to him," another voice spoke. "Listen to my voice now while I can still reach you! My father is still willing to forgive you."

"This is awful," Judas exclaimed. "I'm hearing more than one voice; I must be losing my mind."

"Judas, Judas! Listen to me, Judas!"

"Who is it? I know that voice! Thirty pieces of silver! Oh, what have I done? For thirty pieces of silver, I betrayed my friend, my teacher, the Messiah.

"I do not want the thirty pieces of silver, which are tainted with his blood. Oh, what have I done?"

"Judas! Focus, you betrayed him. It's too late for you. You are mine. Forgiveness is not an option."

"Who is that?"

Death, Reality, and Confusion bombarded Judas, drowning the Messiah's voice and, thus, sealing Judas's fate.

Junior Oakwood, now made into the cross, was in turmoil, and he sought answers that would bring clarity to his chaotic thoughts.

"Teacher, I'm up to the task of bearing you."

"No, Junior!" the teacher replied. "It is not for you that I'm worried. My concern is for the one who sold me to the high priest and the Pharisees.

He is at this moment considering suicide, and it hurts me that I will lose one whom the father gave me! Yet he must die as foretold by my father.

"Thus, I will lose him to Satan and his cohorts, but my father did not say that I could not try. As a matter of fact, my father expects me to try because he has made me this way."

"Is it anything like what you are doing here now?" Junior asked.

"Junior! What makes you think that I'm committing suicide?"

"You have the power to end this with one word, Teacher, but you do not! Instead, you allow these people to beat you and crucify you."

"How astute of you, Junior! I could do all that you have said, but I came for this reason, sent by my father, and I must do what he asks of me! I must allow them to take my life, so that they can be saved."

"Excuse me, Teacher, but that does not make sense," Junior commented. "You said that they must take your life so that they can be saved. Wouldn't it be more logical to live in order to make this happen? Not that I'm questioning you or the father, but it is simply beyond my comprehension."

"Junior, under normal circumstances, the ideal that you propose would be the best choice; however, there are forces—spiritual forces—that ask for this ultimate sacrifice. If my father is willing that I pay this price for their redemption, then I must do his will. Do you understand, Junior?"

"Yes, Teacher, I understand."

For Judas, there was no recourse. The high priest would not see him because he considered him a traitor to his own. Reality and Confusion were successful in blocking out the one person who could save him. And as their success mounted, they applied more pressure on him.

"There is no one who would see you now, Judas," they taunted.

Christ, true to the purpose given him by the father, reached out to Judas to save him. Christ felt the oppressive presence of Reality and Confusion blocking his access. He had already laid down his spiritual power and was as human at this moment as any person could be. The teacher became more human during this episode than at any other moment in his life. The silence at Calvary was palpable as the Messiah prayed for the release of Judas's sins, "The Lord is not slack concerning his promise, as some count slackness, but is long-suffering toward us, not willing that any should perish but that all should come to repentance."[7]

Judas was still alive, and he was remorseful and, thus, savable. At times, he would mention words that came close to acknowledging what he had done. However, every time he seemed to be breaking his bonds, Reality and Confusion held on him with greater determination and intensity. Finally, he succumbed to their urging and hurled himself over the precipice. Death felt a warm glow of victory well up in him.

"Four people all tied together in this historical moment, and I'm the winner," Death congratulated himself. "Judas, you and I have crossed the point of no return, and for you, that is a lonely path to travel."

Before Time, Before Creation: The Teacher's Review of Being Dead

After nine hours of agony on Junior's frame, Christ gave up his spirit. He had wrestled all that time, accumulating all the sins of the world—past, present, and future. He tried to take Judas's and Etchers's sins, but they moved beyond his reach. He finally had all of them that were given up to him, and when he had accomplished this task, he bowed his head.

"It is time. It is finished!"

The strain was beyond even his physical imagination, but his spiritual self knew what it would be like. Man, without the redeemer, would face an unbearable death.

"Junior . . . you must . . . forgive . . . me for laying . . . all . . . this . . . on you . . . even for this short . . . period."

"Master, I'm extremely glad that I could bear you up. After all is said and done, it is the least that I could do for the son of the father!" the cross replied. "It is a privilege to have represented the trees in this endeavor. I will not take the credit for myself only but for my mother and all the other trees down through the ages to this moment and beyond."

"Thank . . . you . . . Junior, and please . . . let . . . the breeze . . . know that I . . . enjoyed his help. It . . . is . . . finished! . . . Man's . . . redemption . . . is . . . paid!"

The Messiah—the teacher—prepared to step down from the cross with his burden of sins. As he began the journey down, Junior sighed, partly from relief and partly from the fact that the teacher had finally died. He groaned as he realized what he had finally missed. While he mused this void, something else came to his mind. Someone touched his mind and whispered, "It is a better thing this is done here today than you or those who are weeping can imagine."

Silence followed the thunder that marked the teacher's death. Into the silence, the awed voice of the guard exclaimed, "Truly, this was the son of God."[8]

Junior's anger ignited at that comment, and he wished that he could convey the magnitude of the evil that was done on that day!

"Don't be angry, Junior, this was planned! Just . . . as . . . creation . . . and . . . redemption . . . was . . . planned, this unfolding . . . even . . . with . . . me, Christ . . . the only . . . begotten son . . . of the . . . father, God. My . . . dying . . . stepping . . . down . . . from the . . . cross . . . and . . . entering . . . Hades to . . . take the . . . keys . . . from Satan . . . was . . . all . . . planned!"

"What? Teacher? But you are dead! How can I still hear you speak? Teacher, what a joy that I was included in the plan, that I was chosen to bear this burden with you to the end."

"Eternity was the beginning and the end," the teacher answered. "Mankind—God's most unique creation, made in his likeness, the ultimate expression of his love—had to be redeemed from the seductive powers of Satan. We arranged it before we made man, knowing that they would fall prey to Satan. Thus, we pledged to us that we would redeem them from him."

"Wow!" Junior remarked. "Still, I am awed that you chose such an end."

"Most . . . assuredly, Junior . . . most assuredly it is! I have willingly done this since before time began. I was chosen to be like man to qualify me to represent humanity. I have lived for this day because I love even as my father loves.

"Junior, if you can see the future of these human beings, then you will understand the benefit of my dying spiritually and physically here today.

"They have a future that the father and myself look forward to enjoying. Believe me, Junior, it is worth it! Satan and Death will face me, and . . . I will be their nightmare."

"Teacher, I would give anything to witness their demise!"

"No, Junior, you would not want to be there. This is a job for me. This is the only way, the way to salvation for all!"

"Teacher, you stand there under all that weight, and here I'm engaging you in conversation. Why don't you put it down if you and I are going to have this conversation?"

"Even if I wanted to, I could not because it is stuck to me for the duration, until I get to Tartarus! I'm trying to get accustomed to the weight before I leave."

"Oh! This is much like what I did when they laid you on me, and then when the sins started piling on you!"

"Exactly, I noticed that you flinched a couple of times as each sin was laid on me. This physical death, this giving up, laying down my life, is something that I willingly do to make sure that as many as those who believe in me will be saved.

"It is a simple but costly endeavor that would allow me to spend all eternity with them! Satan and Death have thought that they are the winners, but I have news for them: they are celebrating prematurely! Hades will never be the same after I walk through and out of it."

"I would still love to be there when you confront those two!" Junior said.

"Junior, Hades—hell—is all fire and brimstone burning for all eternity. How would you fare there?"

"With you as my protector," the cross answered, "I would not have anything to fear!"

"Wrong, Junior. I die as a man, I go to Hades as a man, and feel all the pain that men would feel as men. So wait until I return in three days! Then you can join all mankind in knowing that all that the devil and his cohorts have done is coming to an end.

"In eternity past, I died to this moment. I suffered to this moment, bled and died, but I was spirit. Now, I took on the flesh of man, and I now know that nothing prepares man for this moment.

"For this reason, Satan and Death will suffer eternally. I see they are about to take my body down from you. I see those that I have spent so much valuable time with hurting for me. But they do not have any idea of the pain and anguish that this sacrifice has spared them.

"Oh, sooner or later, they will come to understand as some of them will experience similar ends. I have set the precedence and given them the strength of the Holy Spirit that will be sent by my father, Jehovah God!"

"But you are not yet dead," Junior commented. "You are speaking to me!"

"My body is dead, but my spirit still lives as a man's, to feel as a man will after he has died physically.

"Also, I had to let you know that what you did today was not lost on the father.

"Now I take on all the debt that has been accounted to mankind, to the whole world, in the knowledge that some of them will be saved from the eternal damnation that my father has prepared for Satan and his cohorts.

"This tomb is dark and damp, and I do feel it. My father prepared me for this even in death. I must undergo the same feelings that humanity would feel if I had not died.

"Joseph of Aremathia, I thank you for the loan of your tomb. It will be remembered in history as the dark place where I was entombed temporarily."

"This weight, this sin, this curse, how could mankind bear it?"

"For one man, yes, but for the whole world, past, present, and future, this is an awesome weight."

"It is no wonder there was none who could qualify for this! There was no one who could even try!"

"Death and the sins and curses of this world are awfully heavy even for me. But I will bear it because I see and know the future of those who believe. I see the future of eternity and the beauty that they bring to it.

"I see why the father is bent on saving as many as possible. I see!

"Junior Oakwood, you bore me and the sins of the world. You were made strong by my father with this moment in mind. I thank you. I know that you know that I approve and appreciate what you have done today."

Junior stood there forlornly as they removed the Messiah from him. Junior groaned because he felt so much empathy for the Messiah. The scene that he witnessed in those waning moments of the day left an indelible mark on him. He had just lost his best friend.

"I hope that the father gives you the strength to see this through," Junior said to his master. "In fact, I know that he has because you stood there and showed no hint of discomfort for these sins. Teacher, you should be going now!"

"So long, Junior Oakwood! I should be on my way. I have made this journey so many times through eternity past that it has become second nature to me. I have experienced every word, step, and weight balance—that is, the uniqueness of eternity. It is not time restricted. And so what will be has already been.

"There are no changes—no going back, only forward. For where there is now sadness, it will be replaced by joy. Where there is now pain, it will be made well soon. Where there is now anger and frustration, it will soon be replaced by happiness and assurance.

"Nothing will remain the same as of this day, this hour, this minute, this second, and I thank you, my father, for allowing me this moment!

"If only Judas and the others could understand what awaited them. But Judas should have; he spent many years with me. He saw the miracles that I performed. He knew that I was the Messiah, yet he chose the wrong way.

"So why did he enter that path? Was it the love of money or the love of power? There was no reasoning with him.

"He opened the door to Satan and rejected the gift of eternity. Death does not have the sting that he thought he would have over me. "Now I know! I know why the father wanted me to die for mankind.

Yes! This moment of death is a moment of triumph! It had a purpose!"

The Journey Begins: The Point of No Return—The Night of the First Day in Hades

If Satan had waited and continued his observation of the unfolding scene at the cross, he would have seen the agony, the pain, and the anguish that Christ bore, as each sin made its impression on him who was born for this very moment. He would have seen the Savior of mankind released from the cross under the weight of the sin of man. He would have realized his error, but that was not part of the master's plan.

Death stood watching the Messiah's final moments on the cross. He looked on with a mixture of joy and anxiety. He was happy that he had conquered Christ. Here Christ was dead physically and on his way to Hades.

"He does not have that Spiritual power with which he came from heaven—I know that," Death thought. "His human spirit must be in turmoil now, looking forward to Hades and the ridicule that he will face for all eternity."

Death knew what Satan was thinking before he left the scene. It was written all over the latter's gloating face.

"I can imagine what he is saying and how he is acting right now in Hades!"

Still, there was this anxiety gnawing at Death's unconscious. Death wrestled to bring clarity to this thing that caused him anxiety. Try as he might, he could not, and subsequently, he shrugged it off. At that moment, he looked across at Christ who was looking intently at him, and again, he felt that tension. Christ had a whimsical smile on his face as he turned away and began walking purposefully toward his destination—Hades, Tartarus, and, ultimately, Abraham's bosom.

"I feel happy because I'm victorious over the Messiah. There he is, right in front of me, so what can be gnawing at my mind?"

Death mused. "I have won! Everything went as Satan and I had planned, so what is it? Hmm? Did I do something wrong? Did I overlook something? Ah! I will not let these fuzzy thoughts impede my enjoyment of this occasion."

Little did Death know that his boss Satan was experiencing the same unclear thoughts which dampened the joyous occasion.

"I will say this much," Death reasoned. "Whatever it is, it will not supercede the celebration which will take place in the immediate future in Hades when this so-called Messiah reaches there!"

Still, no matter how Death tried to be happy, a nagging feeling remained with him. Christ knew the source of Death's unease. Death raced on past Christ to join Judas, Etchers, and Adheres on their way to Hades.

Satan believed that a confrontation of some sort should be forthcoming between this self-proclaimed Messiah and Judas. And so he had given specific instructions to let those who died in this situation to "wait for this Messiah to catch up with Judas."

"I know that Satan is always thinking of ways to accomplish some devious act. I would not have thought that the meeting between disciple and teacher would have had any meaning, but Satan does. So I will play along and see what the outcome will be.

"Of course, these two are feeling the effects of what they had experienced just before dying, so they too must be in pain. I do not expect any desire from them to reach their ultimate destination. Look at Judas, he keeps looking back. He is looking for the teacher. He is slowing his approach to Hades so that he can walk the rest of the way with the Messiah."

At the cross, the Messiah prepared to make the journey to Hades. He knew that he would have the company of others with him this day and did not look forward to it. Judas, Etchers, the gatekeeper Mephistopheles, Confusion, and Reality waited for the Messiah.

Adheres knew where he was going, and he knew what—though not all of it—and whom to expect when he got there. He was at once happy and sad about Etchers and the Christ.

Christ reviewed his assignment of transporting the sins to a place of no return where they could do no harm.

"Now, I can fully complete the will of the father," Christ thought, "and bring him the joy of this moment. All heaven is rejoicing although they are sad that it had to happen this way. On the other hand, the occupants of earth will know as time marches on that I—God the father, son, and Holy Spirit—have given them a gift that is unsurpassed from eternity to eternity."

Christ was on his way to Hades to continue the purposed plan of the father.

Darkness followed the Messiah down from the cross as he prepared to make his final journey in the process of man's redemption.

As the son of the father stepped away from the tree, he was heavily burdened with the sins of man. His destination was Hades, but more precisely, Tartarus. He steeled himself for the journey, knowing that it would be tiresome and laden with unfolding dramas to keep his mind off the burden on his shoulders. This fact was his consolation.

"A number of things will be played out today, that my companion travelers will remember for all eternity," Christ said to himself. "I know that Judas is waiting for me, but he will not like my answer to his question. He should have listened when I spoke, instead of worshiping mammon and deceiving others with his rhetoric about the poor. He should have known that the poor were of great concern to me. Oh, if only he stopped to realize it!"

The Savior flinched as he moved along the path of perdition that led to Hades. The nail wounds in his feet made every step he took an experience of searing pain. His constant consolation was the fact that he had pleased the father by accomplishing this much of the plan. Hades lay before him, and soon, he would enter the place of no return. The Messiah stepped forward resolutely; faith in his promised outcome sustained him. Still, Death, Confusion, and Reality lurked, determined to see this through to the end, where—as they did not know it—the Messiah would prevail. Satan's minions could not rewrite the outcome.

Christ could see Adheres a little behind and to the right of Etchers, both in an intense conversation. He saw the divide between them before they were aware of it and smiled sadly at what it meant for him and for them. One of these two will suffer eternal separation from the father, and the other would go on to glory with him. Judas was ahead of these two, moving slowly under the keen eyes of the residents of Hades.

The gate of Hades was clearly visible to the group although it was some distance away. For Adheres, they held the eternal answer for each of those who would enter it this day, but they were simply a spectacle to behold since the master had already promised him a place in with him in paradise.

The decision made by Judas and Etchers while Jesus hung on the cross still pained the Messiah.

"I have looked at Hades from the safety of my father's throne, and this is not a place that I would wish anyone to experience," Christ said to himself. "Judas Iscariot spent three years with me, but he is now on his way to the very place that I came to have him avoid.

"Etchers had an opportunity to change his life, but he did not take it—his last offer of eternity.

"Now here they are, heading for eternal damnation. Too late. They have realized the error of their decision, and they are fighting to reverse it. Now they wait to ask me if there is any hope! How sad!"

As Judas walked with his unwitting companions—Death, Reality, Confusion, and the gatekeeper—he contemplated his plight. Judas knew that only the Messiah could reverse the consequence of his choice. He knew God to be merciful and forgiving, and he hoped to appeal to that nature. He looked at his companions angrily, blaming them for his destination of torment.

"I must ask the forgiveness of God, ask that he free me from this damnation."

The Messiah read his mind and responded with finality: "Too late! It is too late, Judas!"

Judas flinched visibly and quickly looked at his companions for their reaction. He consciously blocked the Messiah's response and chose instead to believe that he could still be redeemed. Judas kept looking back, hoping for that refuge that could only be offered by the Messiah. Judas continued to look behind as he moved forward.

He could see the Messiah coming toward him, laboring under the weight of mankind's sin, although at that time, he did not know that they were sins. He still had his on his back, he realized, and so did Etchers and . . .

"Where is Adheres' back package?" Judas wondered. "Why is he walking along as if under no constraints?

Unbidden, the realization came to him that Christ following behind them . . .

"He is God, the only begotten son of the father—Jehovah God!" Judas exclaimed to himself. "He will soon be here!"

A pang of fear possessed him at the thought that he had before recognized him as such.

"Your kiss of betrayal," Christ addressed Judas, "still lingers on my cheek, Judas!"

"Master!" Judas cried.

Death and the gatekeeper, hearing Judas's cries, looked at him perplexed, thinking "he must be having nightmares already." Thus, they smiled in anticipation.

"Teacher, Master, I did not recognize you buried under that load. How are you doing?"

Judas chose to ignore the pointed statement that Christ made in reference to the kiss. He was not close enough to see the cuts, the bruises, and welts that covered the Messiah's body, but he could tell that Christ was in pain by the way the latter walked. He knew that he was responsible for the teacher's pain.

"I'm responsible for all this. I sold him out," Judas muttered to himself. "But I know that as I speak to him, he will forgive me and rescue me from this hell."

"You are wrong, Judas. You are wrong!"

Still, Judas chose not to hear the damning words. He tried to ignore the crown of thorns on Christ's head, but the enormity of what he had done suddenly hit him. The realization made him cry out even more, bringing more looks of concern and anticipation from his jailers.

"How could I have done this?" Judas said.

After this outburst, he regained his composure. "Would you like some help?" the traitor asked Christ.

Jesus smiled a smile that reflected pain and anguish as he refused the offer. He knew that the offer was attached to an ulterior motive.

"Even in death, Judas," Jesus spoke, "you still try to beguile me. Will you not give up? I do not need any assistance, Judas. I'm well enough to complete this mission to the glory of my father. Judas, this is the reason why I came! This is what I have been trying to tell you and the others for three years! I had to die so that man may not enter this Hades and its eternal punishment!"

Reality was the first to realize that there was an ongoing conversation between Judas and the Christ, although he had not yet reached them.

"I think that he is communicating with the teacher" Reality said explosively!

This statement brought the attention of Death, the gatekeeper, and Confusion, who had melted into the shadows.

As the Messiah trod along, he sensed that darkness was following him, although at a respectable distance. Thus, he said to it in a mind meld, "You will inhabit this path to Hades because no more light will shine here!"

So darkness followed even more discreetly. And the Messiah thought to himself, "This will be an interesting journey."

The Fork in the Road: Etchers and Adheres

Death was fascinated by Adheres and Etchers; he was familiar with their work. The Messiah had a load of sin.

"So where is this thief's sins?" Death wondered. "Something is wrong! But I cannot put my finger on it!"

Just then, the voice seemed to intrude on his mind again. He had felt it before but could not recall its origin. The thoughts hurt his mind as they were expressed.

> It is something that you will never be allowed to decipher, Death. You were never allowed to know it, and for a good reason, it was never any of your business.

Death then became even more interested in Adheres and Etchers, knowing that they had summoned him many times in their lives as they killed innocent people while in the act of robbery. As he watched them, there was a widening gap between them, and he thought that he should know the reason. But it evaded him.

"Hmm? What is going on here?" Death wondered. "They are talking to each other but separating as if they do not want to be beside the other! Ha, finally some controversy is brewing."

Death looked at the three plodding down the path beside him: Judas in front, constantly looking back; Etchers and Adheres behind him having an intense conversation. As Death looked at the latter two, the same feeling that something was amiss crossed his mind again, leaving that blanket of doubt on his mind.

"What is going on? Did I miss something? There is something about these two beside me that raises some unclear thoughts in my mind."

Death shook off the feeling and focused on the joy of his victory. Like his master, he intended to enjoy this auspicious occasion.

The space between the two criminals seemed to grow as Death looked on. They simply seem to move apart without intending to. Both became aware of this phenomenon, and Etchers tried to bridge the gap but could not. Etchers panicked. Death then involuntarily reached out to pull Adheres back but couldn't touch him. In frustration, Death cried out, "I have never lost anyone on this path before! So why can't I even touch him? He is drifting away from me!"

And the anger and frustration that were part of Death's trademark surfaced, causing him to lash out at Reality and Confusion. "Help me! I'm losing him, and I cannot seem to get a grip on him! Come on! Help me!"

No matter how they tried, they could not touch him. Adheres was an arm's length away. Etchers looked on, wanting them to succeed in pulling Adheres back, but they were unsuccessful. This caused Etchers to groan in disappointment. He then said to one particularly, "He was right!"

"I have never lost anyone on this path," Death shot back, "so why now?"

"Yes, you have—many times," Etchers replied. "You have lost some of those that you were accompanying to Hades, but you were not allowed to see them."

"They simply went to Abraham's bosom to await my coming," a voice spoke. "You see, Death, they believed that I would come, and because they did, they were given the opportunity to wait in paradise until I came, something that you assisted me with! Ha-ha!"

"What? I do not understand!"

"You were not meant to understand yet!"

"That voice! I have heard that voice before . . . but . . . where?"

The teacher smiled as Death involuntarily looked behind.

Adheres looked on in sadness as he and Etchers continued to be separated, as if by an invisible hand!

"Funny I should know this, but I keep getting a blank."

Suddenly, a smile of joy broke out across Adheres' face. "I'm free," he said. "I'm free—really—free and on my way to Abraham's bosom!"

Those words had a telling effect on Etchers. But the effect was even more pronounced on the face of Death and his colleagues, as well as on Judas Iscariot.

"We have lost him!" Death said.

"Adheres," the teacher spoke, "as I have told you, you will spend eternity with me in paradise. To achieve that, I took all your sins with me on this journey to Tartarus.

"Sin is like a magnet that keeps its victims on this path, preventing them from making the transition that you have just made.

"Remember, hell was not made for man. Therefore, if sin is not bound to them like these others, they will invariably go to Abraham's bosom.

"Adheres, you will be the last of mankind who believe and confess to me. By taking your sins away, I have helped you avoid the grasp of Death."

Adheres was elated. He responded to the Messiah's last statement by commenting on the reason why he felt so light and unburdened.

"So there is nothing to keep me to this path to those gates up yonder?" Adheres asked. "My sins are on your shoulders, and you have set me free to be redirected to the other side of this place? So Etchers cannot follow me?"

"Adheres," the Messiah answered, "it is man's sin that binds them to this path. While they have sins on their shoulders, they can go no other way but to Hades.

"When I removed your sins, you were no longer bound to the path of Death but, rather, to Abraham's bosom to await my coming. Thus, you naturally are attracted to the right path that leads sinless people to the transition point—Abraham's bosom to await my coming.

"Of course, this location, this paradise that I spoke of with you on the cross, is a temporary place," Jesus said.

"When will this be, Lord?"

"Oh, a few more days and I will come to you and all who wait there for me.

"Now, go, Adheres. You have a job to do. You will be met by the one with whom you will work. I know that you will enjoy paradise, and the people who are waiting there for me. Your appearance there will be the signal that I am on my way.

"Our paths diverge here. I must first pay a visit to the other side of Hades to leave my burden, and you will go to a wonderful place of rest. Forget Judas and Etchers; there is nothing that anyone can do for them."

Adheres recognized the Messiah's pain as he communicated with him. "Why are you in such pain, Teacher? Is it because of the wounds in your side and hands, along with that crown of thorns on your head?"

"Yes, the pain was excruciating," the Messiah answered. "In addition, I have all the sins of the world weighed heavily on me!"

Still, the Messiah but was determined to see it through.

"Adheres, this is something that I must do!" the teacher continued. "It is my choice to do this so that no man who accepts me the way you did back there on the cross would have to go through it too.

"I gladly bear this pain so that man will not have to, if they believe!

"Before the beginning of time, I chose to rescue mankind from their sins, if they believed in me. Etchers, your associate, did not believe in me until it was too late."

The teacher's comment brought sadness and guilt mixed with joy to Adheres. Christ read his mind and said, "Adheres, this is a temporary situation that is almost over. As soon as I reach Hades—the other side to where you are going—it will be over for you and me. And for all who will believe in me from this time on.

"So be joyful and do not feel guilty. It is not what I want for you or any other person. I want you to have joy, joy in the fact that we will be together in paradise, and then in heaven, before my father. Is that not something to rejoice about?"

"Yes, it is, Master, my friend!"

Etchers felt that he would be able to talk the teacher into forgiving him so that he could join Adheres. The teacher knew the painful outcome, and it grieved him that even one might be lost.

"Etchers," the Messiah began, "I had hoped that you would reconsider your ways back there on the cross. You saw the same thing that Adheres saw, so you had the opportunity to do as he did.

"It is now too late for me to help you, Etchers. It is not my will but the father's will that I do, and I have been given strict instructions as to how things must be in order that I will be able to secure the salvation of mankind."

Etchers flinched at the teacher's response. He flinched again when he realized that the distance between him and Adheres continued to widen. He knew then that he would spend eternity in hell.

"Adheres, you were the more violent one when we were alive," Etchers said. "I followed your example, so why am I on my way to hell and you on your way to Abraham's bosom?"

"Oh, Etchers, if you could see what I see and experienced what I have experienced since our parting, you would be awed.

"Now, getting back to your question, I may have been more violent, but you were always the most stubborn, and that is why I am on this side of the divide, and you are on the other.

"I'm on this side of the road watching you, and you still exhibit that stubborn trait."

"Where are you, Adheres?" Etchers asked.

"If you look closer, Etchers, you will see me standing here watching you," Adheres replied. "I don't know why, but the teacher has asked me to stand here in preparation for something that is about to occur. Everything on this side is so beautiful, so refreshing. It is awesome!"

"I miss you, Adheres, old friend!"

"Etchers, you and I were never really friends, just collaborators— joined together in criminal ventures!"

"That hurts, Adheres!" Etchers answered.

"The truth always does, Etchers!" Adheres said. "Etchers, I now realize what true love is. I can see what I think is the most glorious place I could have imagined. It is beautiful and bountiful. It is more beautiful than anything that I could have imagined. It is beyond magnificence!

"To think that God provided this place for us—albeit a temporary place—convinces me of the infinite quality of his love for us. Other than Christ on the cross, the residents of this place seem to be the most loving and wonderful people. They are calling and waving to me! This is heaven, Etchers. This is heaven!

"I only wished that you had listened to my admonition. Even then, you still had the opportunity to convert. But you preferred the laughter of the people, and forgot that you would soon die."

"Adheres, please!" Etchers moaned. "I am in enough pain!"

"Etchers, it is not that I want to remind you of what you have lost; it is that I feel compelled to tell you what you will miss."

"Adheres, I still cannot see you. Where are you? I hear . . . no . . . I feel your voice . . . But I still do not see you. Are you making fun of me again?"

"No, Etchers. You remember what occurred while we were walking down that path? You saw what happened and knew that I was going to where the teacher said I would go," Adheres recalled. "As much as I want to help you, I cannot reach across to you.

"I know what you are thinking, but I cannot help you anymore, Etchers, because there is a chasm between us that I cannot traverse, and neither can you.

"However, if you look in the general direction from where you can sense me, you can see what the teacher intends—something to take with you as you go through those gates up ahead of you. Good-bye, Etchers."

Judas had been observing the intensity of the conversation of Adheres and Etcher. Adheres and Etchers had been a solid pair, but for some reason, Adheres moved off from Etchers and was now standing off there with a chasm between them.

"Why did they separate anyway?" Judas wondered.

Judas and Etchers began to communicate with each other. Perhaps they could console each other on this journey.

"Why are you here? Weren't you a disciple of the teacher? Etchers asked Judas.

"Why are you here when your friend is over there?" Judas asked back.

Despite their need for each other, their first attempts at conversation were barbs, words that pierced each other. Unconsciously, they agreed that hurting each other was unproductive, so they walked silently side by side.

Meanwhile darkness continued treading at a discreet distance so as not to impede the Messiah's progress. He knew what was happening and felt a loneliness creep into his being.

"What is this?"

Mephistopheles howled in anger at the apparent loss of Adheres while Reality looked on in frustration. Both knew that there was something different about Adheres but could not identify the change nor its origin.

Yes, both Mephistopheles and Reality knew that Adheres had gone to the cross to die for his misdeeds, along with his companion Etchers. But something occurred on the cross that had since kept them guessing. Adheres had come down that cross a different person from the one that went up. Look at his companion—nothing about him has changed!

Mephistopheles and Reality began to feel that gnawing awareness of a truth that kept escaping them. And so a trio of souls came to that infamous crossroad that divided Hades.

Death was unaware of the division in the path to perdition. This path was divided, with one side leading to paradise—Abraham's bosom—known only to Etchers and Christ. And so for the first time, he was allowed to see what really went on since man began to die, starting with Abel, Adam and Eve's son.

"How can I explain this to Satan?" Death began to focus on the other two humans—Judas Iscariot and Etchers. "I will not allow what just happened to Adheres to occur again. I will be more observant, more watchful."

Judas was crestfallen as he saw the unfolding drama of separation. Adheres was on his way to Abraham's bosom, and knowing what it meant, Judas sulked in silence.

"He was right all along!" thought Etchers. "I should have been open to salvation. So this is what it is all about, this salvation that

I have lost. More important, I seem to have robbed a number of people of that opportunity."

Just then, a shadow blotted out the light. Judas looked up and saw the Messiah burdened with the load of sin approaching.

"Master! Lord! Messiah! Please, be merciful to me and forgive me. I realize that I betrayed you, and I'm really sorry! Please, give me another chance. Have mercy on me! You know that I worked hard for you while I lived!"

Christ's response had an eternally chilling effect on Judas Iscariot. "I do not know you. You betrayed me for thirty pieces of silver! It is too late for forgiveness; you must face the consequences of your choice."

Death and Etchers were dismayed at the unfolding of this drama. It was not the outcome they'd imagined, and it was not the news that Satan wanted to hear.

"Did I or the master underestimate this teacher? Death pondered. "Is there something that we did not calculate into the formula to defame him?"

Judas collapsed under the judgment. No sooner had he sunk to the ground than he was prodded to his feet by Death and Reality. He was not going to be allowed the luxury of unconsciousness, not when faced with presenting a bad report to Satan.

"Judas," Jesus asked, "do you remember the story that I told the Pharisees about the rich man and Lazarus? You will meet the rich man in Hades. He will be there crying in pain that he must bear for all eternity."

"Eternity, Teacher? . . . Eternity . . . eternity?"

"The punishment that the rich man received is the punishment that is meted out to all who have chosen the way he chose. While he was alive, he had many opportunities to change but did not.

"Judas, like him, you had numerous opportunities to change your lifestyle.

"Those choices brought you to this time and place. Now, here you are, and it is too late!"

Nothing could have condemned Judas more as, finally, the sentence was pronounced by Christ. The Messiah resumed the journey with his awesome load, surrounded by fellow travelers Judas, Etchers, and the demon's cohorts.

Mephistopheles looked more pleased as they drew nearer to the gates of hell. He may have lost Adheres, but he still had claimed a significant harvest. He gloated at the Messiah's discomfort, but Christ kept on walking, unperturbed by the antics of those around him. He knew the outcome.

Mephistopheles tried to engage the Messiah in conversation but failed. From that moment on, Mephistopheles kept silent. Still, as Judas looked at him, he seemed pleased. Judas looked from Christ to the demon, hoping for something to occur.

Perhaps, Judas thought, there would be one last opportunity for the master to come to his aid. He kept thinking, maybe Jesus would reconsider his position; after all, he is the Messiah, the son of God. He has the power to do what he wants.

Christ turned to Judas and corrected him. "No, Judas. This is not my will but my father's. Do you understand? I cannot change what the father has spoken before time began. I must complete the mission that he has asked of me! For this reason, I do not need any assistance from either of you! I must do this alone!"

Though Mephistopheles and Death had brought Judas and Jesus together, there was to be no final attempt at redemption. Adheres stood on the other side of the void and watched their efforts to obtain atonement. Hope for Judas's redemption meant hope for Etcher's.

Still, the party lagged, dragging their feet on the journey to Tartarus, Christ with the weight of sin heavy on his back, Judas and Etchers realizing that there was no hope. Adheres, realizing that he still had a part to play in the situation, reached out to Christ,

"Teacher? Lord, why am I still standing here?"

"You are about to enjoy the pleasure of the path that you are on," Jesus replied, "so stand still, and you will see!"

"Thank you, Lord."

"What is this?" exclaimed Etchers. "What's . . . going . . . on?"

He had begun to feel the intense heat of Hades. He had felt heat in the dessert, in the place where the Messiah went to be alone for forty days and nights, but not like this! Suddenly, a light appeared, and it illuminated Adheres briefly.

"Adheres!" called out Etchers. "Can you hear or see me?"

"Yes, Etchers, I can both hear and see you! I have been watching you ever since we parted company.

"Why have you stopped talking to me?" Etchers asked. "You know that it was an opportunity for us to communicate with each other before we went to our separate destinations."

"Oh, I did not want to give you false hope, knowing that there is nothing I or anyone can do for you," Adheres explained. "Be on your way now; I 'm waiting to be escorted to paradise."

When Adheres said that last part of the sentence, sadness overtook him momentarily. Etchers stood silently for a moment; then he resolutely turned his attention to the road ahead.

The pain and anguish that welled up inside Judas burst forth in a wail that drew the attention of Etchers, as well as Adheres, who was still visible on the other side of the road. Each recognized in that hopeless cry the soul of the eternally dammed. Judas looked in the direction of Adheres; regret overwhelmed the former, and he sank to his knees in hopeless despair.

Suddenly, the light appeared again. This time, Judas caught a glimpse of Adheres in the presence of two angels, who had come to escort him to Abraham's bosom.

"It is about to begin, Adheres," Jesus spoke. "It is about to begin, and I want everyone on this side of the road to witness it."

"Messiah, that light . . . it was so bright, so beautiful. What was it?"

"Oh, it is the light of the angels who are standing beside you."

"Angels, Teacher? I do not see any angels!"

"You will," Jesus answered. "I asked them to remain invisible for a while; then you will see them too."

With all hope squeezed from him, Etchers stumbled along as the rest of the group began to move again. This time, his eyes were fixed on the spot where he first saw the light.

"I need to see those lights again. I do not know why, so don't ask me. But I need to see them again!" Etchers said.

"To tell you the truth," Adheres responded, "I too need to see them again also. It is as if I need some kind of confirmation, or something that I cannot explain! It is as if I will never see such beauty again!"

It was a lifeline to an eternity they would never know.

Adheres stood rooted to the path that seemed to rise, separating from the other side, and he experienced a moment of fear. How will I get to my destination? he wondered. As soon as the thought entered his mind, the Messiah reached out to reassure him.

"You will not have to walk, Adheres. You will be carried up and over it. The two angels standing beside you will take you to Abraham's bosom, but it is not yet time. At my bidding, the angels will make themselves known."

Adheres was overjoyed. He was truly on his way to paradise! He looked at Etchers regretfully, still unwilling to release his associate. I must at least distract him, he thought to himself, from the reality that faces him.

"You can do no more for him," Jesus reminded Adheres. "Let him go!"

"Yes, Lord."

Adheres had been contemplating his blessing, having called on the teacher while they were on the cross. What he received from Christ as he hung on the cross had caused him to change the way he thought about the sins that he had committed. And so as he looked at the teacher going down the road, he now saw things in a different light.

Adheres felt things that he had never allowed to influence him before. Thus, it was with this new mind-set of caring that he looked at the teacher, trudging along with this enormous burden of sin—man's sins.

As Adheres watched the teacher under the strain of sins and the obvious pain that he was feeling, he felt the urge to reach out and help him. This was an awesome change that had occurred in his life. Thus, involuntarily, he reached out in his mind to console the Messiah. Sensing his concern, Christ reminded him of the reason for this temporary suffering.

"This is a temporary situation for me, Adheres. It will soon be over, and man will be free from Death and Satan. I alone must conclude this task, if you are to enjoy Abraham's bosom and all eternity with me. Do you understand, Adheres?"

"Yes, Teacher. Lord, I'm thankful that you have come to this plateau of understanding because it is a confirmation that man will feel and believe this way also. So thank you!"

"I can see that you have taken on my attributes, Adheres," the Messiah said. "It is a pleasure to see them operating in you. But know this: I do it so that you and I and all those who believe can spend eternity in joy and peace, free from the devil and his cohorts.

"More important, Adheres, you do not know half of what is in store for you and all who believe that I'm the only begotten son of the father—God. I am Messiah, the Messiah!"

Christ was coming abreast of Judas Iscariot, Etchers, and their company from hell. While Adheres was saying good-bye to Etchers, Christ thought of his attempts to save Judas from this end of all ends. Christ had never wanted this for him, although he knew before even him, Judas, that this would be the result of his actions.

"While there is life, there is always hope," Jesus said. "But for you, Judas, hope ran out when you took your own life and died."

Adheres' thoughts then wandered to all those times that he and Etchers were together. He thought that of all the people that he had known, Etchers would have been the one to join or become agreeable to certain ideologies. He was the one who suggested that they go and see what was going on with the baptizer. He was the one who became animated with what the baptizer had said. Thus, he should have been the one to believe the Christ!

So why is he the one who is on the way to Hades, while I'm the one going to Abraham's bosom? Adheres wondered. Now he is seeking companionship from the one whom he gave up—the Christ.

This was so ironic; both had the same opportunities.

Judas chose to walk even more closely now with Etchers because suddenly a fear and dread descended on him from nowhere. Simultaneously, Etchers began wondering why he began dreading the next steps that he had to take and was glad when Judas sidled up to him. It was as if both felt the need for each other's company without knowing why.

The Messiah, on the other hand, saw their action and knew that the dread of hell had descended on them, but they did not know it yet. The Messiah walked in expectation because he witnessed the two humans' reaction.

Meanwhile, Mephistopheles looked longingly at the gates that loomed in the distance. Not so far now, Mephistopheles thought to himself, and this Messiah will walk through forever. These gates will hold him for eternity.

Christ smiled as the thought ran through Mephistopheles' mind.

Not so! It is not so, gatekeeper, Jesus thought to himself. I will have the last laugh because my father made a covenant with me that he will be with me and would not let my body rot in the grave. He never lies! Any minute now Death, any minute now, Mephistopheles, you will all see what has evaded you for so long. Any minute now, Adheres, and you will be caught up by angels who will take you to Abraham's bosom. Any minute now, and the last soul to pass this way to paradise will be taken along this path to Abraham's bosom."

Suddenly, there was music. Suddenly, there was an ambience that permeated the area around Adheres and those who were on their way to the gates of Hades. Two angels appeared out of nowhere and stood on both sides of Adheres. Adheres stood there transfixed, as was the group on the other side of the void.

Judas was the first to speak involuntarily, in a manner that he had not intended because he still held some vestige of hope that before he would go through those gates, the Messiah would change his mind about him.

"This is not happening!" Judas murmured. This is wrong! I should be over there with him, the thief, and not being reminded of what I have lost.

Jesus, who stood a little behind them, couldn't resist an answer to Judas. "That is not all, Judas. There is more to come for you!" Then the Messiah added, as if to no one in particular, "Let it begin!"

Jesus then looked turned to Death, who was caught in a fight with himself as he saw the apparition that stood beside Adheres. Death was fighting with something that came awake in his mind once more but still could not recognize it.

"This is fun!"

And so the Christ looked in anticipation, not so much for what else was about to unfold but for the effect it had on each of them in the party in front of him.

"What is it?" Death asked. "What is going on in my mind? I'm not one to forget easily!"

Suddenly, Death knew what was happening before his eyes: Adheres was on his way to Abraham's bosom!

"How is it that I have never noticed this side path before, even after so many deaths? All this times, something kept me from knowing or remembering, but I ought to because those who are over there have also died!

"I can remember when I went to collect Abel," Death continued, "the first man to die at the hands of his brother Cain. But to this day I cannot recall what happened in those moments. Is this what happened to him?"

Death realized at that moment that all the people who had died and transported to Abraham's bosom were blocked out from his mind. But now, for some unknown reason, he was allowed to see it all and remember! With that thought, Death looked back at the Messiah and realized that he had something to do with it. Up to that point, the only persons in the group that really saw the angels were the two humans and Christ on that side of the void and, on the other side, Adheres.

The light that shone on Adheres' side of the road was intense and hurtful to the demons and humans alike.

"Oh! The light! This is an unreal light! Where is it coming from?" Death asked no one in particular.

Suddenly, the two angels that had appeared on the side of the path that Adheres took became visible to Death. He was astounded, and his first thought was that they had come to join them in Hades.

Then Christ whispered into his mind, "Never, Death. Look more closely. You will see the sight that has evaded you for thousands of years."

Death, for the first time, had no words. Not only were these angels appearing there and him not knowing it. More important, he recognized both of them. Michael. Gabriel. Death recognized Michael whom he had fought so many times. They fought over Moses' body because Satan wanted him and countless others whom he tried to take before their time.

"I remember you, Michael! I . . . remember . . . you!"

"Gabriel!" the angel said.

"You have Lucifer's trumpet. I recognize it!" Death said.

Michael smiled dauntingly as he looked over at Death, and Gabriel waved his trumpet to him.

"This is a special occasion for me. The Messiah asked and the father had granted this before time began!"

"He wanted you to see how much you have lost, and I know that you will also lose more before he is through with you!"

"Gabriel," Death said, "Satan would like to have a conversation with you. You have been playing his trumpet, haven't you?"

Gabriel took out his trumpet in response to Death's inquiry and lit up the air—stagnant as it was—with a beautiful piece of music. Death quailed at the sound, as did Mephistopheles, Reality, and Confusion, who continuously remained in the darkness, but the light uncovered them. The group was much shaken at the sight that was presented to them from the other side of the road.

Heaven rejoiced; Abraham's bosom rocked with joy; Adheres inhaled and exhaled pure ecstasy of unabridged joy and happiness. The music that came from Gabriel's trumpet was like a whole orchestra with thousands of instrument. It awakened emotions that played real music to some and havoc on others. Adheres was jubilant, while Etchers screamed in agony from the pain the music caused.

Christ was overjoyed as peace washed over him in human-spirit form. At that moment, he forgot the pain that he was bearing. The music was a refuge for him for a fleeting moment, reminding him of what he could expect when it was all over. Man's redemption was paid in full. Death cringed, and Mephistopheles looked longingly at the gates of hell, wanting to run full speed toward it to get away from the sensation that Gabriel's music was having on him. Yet they could not move; they were held bound, hoping that Gabriel would soon finish.

What they did not know was that Satan in Hades heard the sound of the trumpet and recognized it as his. He too felt the pain that the music reverberated throughout the confines of hell. Still, Gabriel continued to rock the group's boat, so to speak.

Death became subjugated for the first time as he listened, spellbound by the music that emanated from Gabriel's trumpet.

"I would like this music to cease. It reminds me too much of heaven, something that I really do not want to remember. Furthermore, I have never reacted in this manner to the music that came forth from this trumpet.

"Why did Lucifer leave it behind when he left?"

The traveling party, the residents of Abraham's bosom, and all of Hades heard and felt the impact of this music. They were caught in its power. Satan, in the process of enjoying his so-called victory, was caught unawares by the sound of the trumpet. He froze, not only because he knew that it was his trumpet that was being blown (he had brought music to heaven on many an occasion with this instrument, which the father had made for him). Satan froze because the music now brought pain, pain which he had never experienced since he landed on earth, having been thrown unceremoniously out of heaven. He had no control over the circumstances of his falling then, and he had none now. The sound of the trumpet in his ears kept him spellbound and under its ruling. He was going nowhere, and he knew it.

"Oh! Who, where, why?" Satan groaned. The words kept tumbling out of his mouth without him even knowing that he was posing such questions.

The demons around him looked at him as they too writhed under the pain of the music. Why does he ask these questions? some of them were thinking. It was his trumpet that he blew every morning in heaven.

Long ago, Satan would go up to the North Mountain and blow this trumpet. Out of it would come such sweet music. But today, it was being blown—not by him—and it brought pain. Will this pain not go away? Every resident of Hades heard it and was hurt, while in Abraham's bosom, it brought such joy, unadulterated, unspeakable joy.

The devil had no answer for what was transpiring at that moment. So when a question was posed by one of the demons, as to the reason for the trumpet being blown in the vicinity of Hades, Satan had no answer.

"I guess that Gabriel have decided to join us," Satan quipped. And a wisp of a smile crossed his face.

The devil knew that could not be so, but he had to say something that could keep him from losing face before his underlings. However, no sooner had he said the words than he started screaming, and it went on for as long as the trumpet blew. In that moment, those who were with him cringed in the pain even more. They also realized that he, Satan, could feel pain and could be hurt.

Satan saw the looks that were directed at him and could not, in that moment, do anything about it. He had lost it in those seconds of pain that seemed to last an eternity. I must regroup, he thought. I cannot allow these to think that they could hurt me, that they have some kind of hold over me.

And so Satan tried to straighten up under the pressure of the music that wailed in his ears.

"Wow! I did not realize how much power that trumpet had over others!" Satan said.

The statement seemed to have a calming effect over those who heard him. Still, the devil was far from confident that they bought his explanations. He knew that Gabriel would never join him. He also knew that the trumpet was designed in such a manner that it could cause pain to the right people—those who were against the father, the Holy Spirit, and his son, the Christ.

The moment of the trumpet's sound left a taste of uncertainty in the devil's mouth. And although it stopped after a moment, which for him was like an eternity of pain, the devil knew that things will not be the same for a long time.

Oh boy, did I lose control of my underlings? the devil wondered.

The question, of course, was posed to himself, but those that looked at him had another opinion—although they would not let him know it. Momentarily, he forced the celebration to continue, knowing that he had to regain control of the situation immediately.

Again, Christ under his burden of pain and suffering smiled. Death and Confusion saw it and wondered. This too left some doubt in their minds as to how much control they had over this party, particularly the teacher.

"Oh no! Death, you cannot believe that the father would have allowed Lucifer to take that trumpet with him, now can you?"

Death whirled around, looking at Christ. "You spoke into my mind!"

"Yes, and I have been doing it ever since I embarked on the road to perdition," Jesus answered.

"Ahh!" Death said. "So this is it! You have been putting me through the wringer, so to speak, since Calvary?"

"Yes!"

But Death could do nothing about what he had just learned. Meanwhile, his other companions looked at him with concern because they did not hear what he had just heard.

"Are you going berserk?" they asked

The gatekeeper was able to get out as he strained under the pressure of Gabriel's music. Death's response was a withering look that spoke volumes of his intent. If only he could move. The gatekeeper decided not to confront Death anymore.

To the party on their way to Hades and Tartarus, it was pure, unadulterated agony, except for the Messiah whose face reflected his true feelings, his emotion. The smile radiated from his face and eased the agony that he knew he had to bear for mankind's sake.

Judas quailed even more than before. He had heard of Gabriel's trumpet but had never heard it played. To hear it at such a moment as this was the ultimate of distress. So Judas dropped to his knees in more pain than he thought that he could feel.

His thoughts ran rampant now as he envisioned what it would have been like to hear this same trumpet played under different circumstances while he was alive.

It would have made so much difference as to how I acted, he thought.

That thought was interrupted by the Messiah saying, "You would have done nothing different, Judas. You would have done nothing different."

"Teacher, how do you know that?"

"You ask such a question, Judas? Have you not heard me say before that I and my father are one?[9]

"Therefore, in my human form, he reveals to me all things that I should know, and I knew that you would not act any differently. Do you still not remember the story of the rich man and Lazarus the beggar?"

"There was so much to be learned from that lesson, but obviously, you did not!"

Etchers was no different from Judas and the others in the party. His agony became a hundredfold as he writhed under the pain of the trumpet.

"Stop . . . it . . . stop . . . it! Please . . . stop . . . it!" Etchers groaned.

Adheres, preparing to leave with his companions, looked at Etchers and saw his reaction, and shook his head. The joy that he felt as the music reverberated throughout the area was tempered by the sight of Etchers writhing from the pain alongside Judas.

"Those two, of all people, had such an opportunity but wasted it."

And as if on command, both Michael and Gabriel lifted Adheres on their wings. Judas saw it and felt his pain increase more than he had thought that he could bear, like none that he had ever experienced.

"Ahh! What? Why? Where . . . are . . . they . . . taking . . . him?" Judas asked.

The questions flew out of Judas's mouth in rapid succession. It was not that he didn't know but that it took him by surprise because he had often heard the teacher mention it. Of all the things that had happened to him in the last day, this was the most painful.

Judas saw his destiny in that bright shining moment and knew that he had really lost the most precious thing that had ever been offered to him. Reality had done a number on him. Thanks to his master, Satan. Right before his eyes, Judas saw what he had thrown away and the prospect of what lay ahead for him.

"Not yet, Judas. There is more to come for you, and you will feel the effects of this episode that you just experienced more than ever!" Jesus spoke to himself.

Death looked like something or someone had a strangling hold on his neck and was squeezing the life out of him. He was immediately pale, as if he had never experienced sunlight or the fires of Hades. He felt a tug on his arm and swung furiously in the direction of the assault—or so he thought. Only to find the gatekeeper holding on to him in a very distraught manner.

"Have you ever seen this before?" Death asked the gatekeeper.

"You are Death. You must have experienced it before, haven't you?" the gatekeeper asked back.

"Of course, I have!" Death lied. "But why did you ask, and why are you pulling me apart, Mephistopheles?"

The gatekeeper realizing, how stupid he looked hanging on to Death, let go sheepishly and said, "I just thought that . . . never . . . mind!" he said.

Etchers look at the spectacle and couldn't hold back from crying. There were no tears coming from his eyes, yet he sobbed as he saw the angels lift Adheres on their wings. There was no consoling him, and at that moment, he knew that he had to approach the teacher hoping that he could redeem him.

"Oh, there must be something that the Messiah can do for me!" he said. "Maybe he will have mercy on me and allow me to go over to the other side.

"I do not mind if I have to walk all the way to Abraham's bosom—it will be worth it!"

Christ read his mind and knew that more than ever the former thief wanted to ask him for forgiveness as a way out of his dilemma.

Death still fought an invisible fight with his mind and began to ask, "Is this what has been on the fringes of my consciousness, bothering me? No, there must be more to it!

"What did the Messiah say to Adheres? And more important, what did Adheres say to him?"

Now Death was really troubled but made a promise to himself that he would not allow his charges to see that something troubled him. However, he did not fool Mephistopheles because he kept looking furtively at him when he was not looking.

He is lying to me, Mephistopheles thought to himself. "He has never seen this before!"

And no sooner did he say it under his breath than the Messiah confirmed it.

"Of course he is lying!" Christ said. "He was never permitted to see this! And you, although you have been close enough at the gates to see it, neither did you."

"Messiah?"

"Yes, Mephistopheles. Your mind is open to me, as his is!"

Mephistopheles now looked at Death with hate, conveying his feeling for him who had lied so blatantly to him.

Adheres on the wings of the angels saw the reaction from the party on the other side of the path and felt a pang of guilt for Etchers who was crying continuously. Still, he and the angels stood there, not moving. It was then that he realized that the Christ was conferring with them. Adheres wondered what the Messiah told them.

It is interesting that even the angels obey him, Adheres thought. "How come mankind did not realize this? Did they not know with whom they lived and ridiculed all these years? Their eyes were blinded, and their ears stopped because they are a headstrong people. Yet the father loved them enough to allow his only begotten son's death and this journey to occur so that they can be saved if they believe.

"Teacher, Messiah, Lord! I thank you for my salvation!"

The Messiah then spoke to the angels, and Adheres heard every word.

"Do not move yet," Christ said. "This is a moment that this group must see, and it must sink into their now-vivid memory.

They will never see it again! This is the first and last time for them because I will conquer both of them, thus allowing me to set the captives of Abraham's bosom free."

Etchers looked at Adheres on the wings of the angels and started crying even more, shaking convulsively. "What a fool I have been! A few lousy moments of influence by the crowd, and I sealed my fate. Now I'm trying to escape what lies ahead!"

Time stood still in that moment of beauty for Adheres and Christ. On the other hand, the picture that was being painted stroke by stroke, layer by layer on the minds of the Hades-bound group was indeed done so deliberately and with indelible colors that would not be removed for all eternity.

Judas stood there, forlornly lost in thought, knowing that this would have been his portion had he not become materialistic.

"Materialism does not work, does it?" Jesus spoke.

Judas turned to see the teacher watching him intently. The teacher seemed to say, "Remember what you did to me and to yourself!"

"As you remember this moment through all eternity," Jesus spoke, "also remember that I gave you every opportunity to change, even up to the moment when you decided to and did kill yourself."

Judas wept!

"Thirty pieces of silver, Judas! That is what you sold your soul for! It is an eternity of punishment, more than you will ever imagine.

"I really do not know why you allowed Satan to take such a grasp of you. Now, you must reflect on this choice for eternity!"

It seemed an eternity before the angels and Adheres moved even an inch. Finally, the angels turned to head the other way, and Adheres took that moment to wave good-bye to Etchers. And then they were gone. Christ had given the angels their leave to take Adheres home, and they obeyed.

This left Etchers in a very somber, very forlorn, and evil mood, after which he eventually stopped crying. That gave Death a measure of pleasure.

"At least three out of four is not bad, but the real prize is now here with me," Death declared.

"I'm not your prize Death, and I thought that by now you would have realized it!

"You are not in control. You were never in control. And worse, now you will lose even more of whatever control you thought that you had!"

Mephistopheles smiled wickedly, and Death turned to face him. Softly, he spoke to Mephistopheles, which sent a chill running through him.

"Why are you laughing, Meph? Is there something funny that I failed to see or understand?"

The gatekeeper knew that when Death shortened his name, he was in a foul mood and not to be crossed.

"No, Death," the gatekeeper quickly replied. "I was only thinking that if he was in control as he said, why is he still heading toward the gate of no return?"

The answer seemed to make Death feel a little better, and they both turned toward the gate.

The gatekeeper pondered what he had just seen. Thus, as he strode in front of the Hades-bound group, he kept thinking of it. "Has this been going on all this time—and I've not seen it?

"Could it be that I—we, this place—is in such a vulnerable position that these angels have been doing this, and we do not know it?

"And what about Death? He has been guiding them along the path, and he should have known it. But he said nothing when these people disappeared from him! Not once did I hear him say anything!

"Satan is going to be mad if he ever hears about this."

This was the gatekeeper's constant thought as he trudged toward the gate. "Satan should know about this. It could be that I may be rewarded!"

Christ smiled as he walked along with them. Darkness still followed at a discrete distance.

"I do not want to be on the wrong side of this Messiah! I see what he can do!"

The group remained in a flux after the occurrence with the angels and Adheres. But Etchers felt it more than the others. He had not realized how attached he and adheres had been until he saw his associate taken away.

"Now he is gone, carried off by angels to where I do not and may not know."

"Obviously, they are taking him to paradise. That was what the teacher told him, 'This day, you will be with me in paradise.' I will remember those words for all eternity!"

"Teacher," Etchers said, turning to Christ, "please forgive me and set me on the path to Abraham's bosom! I won't mind walking it!"

"Sorry, Etchers. You have lost your opportunity to be on that path. It is a path that one chooses while he is alive!

"You are dead, so that makes you ineligible to go there! And believe me, you do not know how sorry I am that I must say these words to you."

Etchers wept. His crying was one of hopelessness that cannot be circumvented. He was eternally doomed and knew it in that instant.

The teacher, Christ, had not wanted Etchers or Judas to end up on the wrong path leading to Hades. But deep in his heart, he knew that Judas would betray him and end here. It would have been good if they, Judas and Etchers, had responded to his voice and made the same decision as Adheres.

They did not listen, and so here they are, on the path of perdition that leads to Hades, Jesus thought. "For Judas, although he does not yet know it, his journey does not end there! He goes on to Tartarus where he belongs for betraying the son of the father!

"If Etchers had listened and accepted then when he arrived in paradise, he and Adheres would have had a wonderful time discussing it.

"On the other hand, Judas would not have been here but preparing to go forth and preach the good news of his pending second coming. What a pity," Jesus said to himself.

"Judas, there is a place prepared for you that is far worse than what anyone else in this group can fathom. You are going down into the pit of Tartarus with me! I had hoped that you would not go this way, although when I called you to join me, I knew who you were."

Between Judas and Etchers, it was hard to determine which of them felt worse. Each was saddened by what they now know and what was to come that they would miss. Etchers would constantly remember what he could have received if he had followed Adheres' approach on the cross. Similarly, Judas, waiting to talk to him, found out how much he too had lost. Still, I know that he does now have an idea about that.

The teacher felt the sorrow that came at the cost of these two who were now following him.

"Father," Jesus said, "I tried to win them over, but Satan had his claws so deeply imbedded in them, using guile and greed. He clouded their minds from what is true. They could not see beyond Reality.

"Satan manipulated them using their weaknesses against them. He will pay, and more so now that he has given me the added reason, these two lost souls!"

Etchers now realized what he had been offered and not taken. Consequently, his demeanor was characteristic of his life. He felt mean and evil and was not about to be consoled by anyone. Not that there was anyone to console him.

Death, Reality, and the gatekeeper watched Etchers as he changed, becoming more evil, more anxious, striking out at no one in particular. Christ, as he walked in front of them, listened as the scene unfolded and felt some pity that he would not allow them to see.

Judas had come to the realization of his mistake and felt a certain pain that went beyond the self-inflicted pain of hanging oneself. And so as the teacher continued his trek before these two and their escort, he knew that they had lagged, hoping to speak to him. But now they found out that it was a futile attempt. Judas and Etchers had both thought, He is the answer to my problems, so I must speak with him. He is Messiah!

"You made a choice that became a reality for you," Jesus addressed Judas and Etchers. "Do you not recognize Reality walking beside you? He had a hand in your decision making? He brought to you the ideals that you now know, mean nothing, are not substantive. And because you chose material over spiritual, you forfeited any opportunity to call me Master.

"I'm sorry for you, Judas, because you will be judged more harshly than others who did not have the privilege that I gave you."

Still, Judas would not give up trying. If I see him face-to-face and away from this group, he will forgive me and help me, was his thought. But it availed him nothing.

Judas said something that was directed to the teacher although he was still some distance ahead of him. But for the first time, the teacher was so lost in thought in preparation for what was ahead that he failed to respond to Judas's question.

"Where is he going?" Judas's question came again!

"Are you referring to Adheres, Judas?" Jesus said.

"Yes! Why is he going in that direction? I did not see a split in the road."

"Oh, there is a split in the road; that is why you are on this left side and he is on the right. It is only natural!"

"Why?" Judas asked.

"He responded to my invitation while he was on the cross," the teacher explained. "He asked me to forgive him and remember him when I come into my kingdom. I told him that on this day, he would be with me in paradise! And he will be! I thought that Etchers had explained that to you."

That last part of the conversation did more to cause Judas pain than anything that occurred to him that day! Needless to say, Etchers was in even more pain as he saw his longtime friend part ways with him to go in the direction that the teacher had confirmed to Judas.

I will really miss his companionship in the days ahead, Etchers thought, because we have been together for so long.

"Etchers, I hate to tell you this, but I prefer here than where you are going. I will not allow you to even think of blaming me for your mistake. You had the same opportunity as I did, but you refused it."

Darkness knew what had transpired along the path to perdition. He had witnessed it many times. He presumed that Death and Mephistopheles had known about it too. I was wrong, he quietly realized.

Tartarus

Judas and Etchers were near to the gates. In anticipation of the new members in Hades, Mephistopheles tried to race past the teacher, superceding them and leading them as he had done so many times previously. However, he could not supercede the Messiah. As he approached the gates, they opened as if by an invisible hand.

Mephistopheles is the gatekeeper, and this is his main function. He did not get to the gate in time, yet it opened and allowed the Christ through!

"What is this?" the gatekeeper asked. The question came unintended into his mind and out of his mouth. He was appalled at the occurrence. "Did he touch the gate? I did not see him touch the gate! So why did it respond obviously to his approach? Hmm . . ."

Consternation grew on Mephistopheles' face, but he tried to hide it from the other members of the group. Furthermore, he was intrigued by their lagging and standing there and not being propelled by Death to enter this one-way gate. Death, on the other hand, had noticed the automatic response of the gate but said nothing as he looked at Mephistopheles.

He is bewildered too, the gatekeeper thought. "He does not know what happened, even as I do not!"

It was an unusual situation, which his attention. But as he looked closer, he saw that both Death and Reality were gloating over the coup that Satan had pulled off this day. Or so he thought. They had effectively destroyed the mission of Christ . . . Or so they thought.

Mephistopheles, with a gleeful look in his eyes, turned and spoke to Christ, who had now started walking down the path that led to the middle of Hades. The devil was still trying to irk Christ. But Christ paid no attention to him; he simply kept on walking.

"Well, Messiah?" the gatekeeper began. "What happened? Did you lose something that you are to collect here, and with this load no less?" He said it with a certain amount of satisfaction wringing in his voice.

"Actually, Mephistopheles, I did not lose anything that I couldn't find if I wanted to!"

The teacher's answer to Mephistopheles intrigued the latter, who obviously did not understand what had been said.

"What I have lost," Jesus added, "I'm on my way to find." Again the demon gatekeeper could not understand and gave up trying. "If you are looking for my boss Satan, he is expecting you."

And the teacher's response made him even more uncertain about how to take it. "Hmm. Well, he will have to wait until I have deposited this load."

"Yes, what is that . . . that you are carrying anyway?" The gatekeeper asked. "It seems rather heavy!"

"It is, but it is something that I gladly carry because of its importance."

"Nothing is important down here," Mephistopheles complained. "Not even this hypocrite Judas that kept me waiting at the request of Satan."

Christ was having fun with him as a distraction from the pain that he felt all over his body. However, Mephistopheles did not realize it, so Christ said, "Go tell your master that I have arrived; he will understand."

Judas, thinking that he could make some points and hopefully change his situation, chimed in to tell the gatekeeper what Christ meant. Nonetheless, he did not get the opportunity because Christ commanded him to be quiet. And that was the end of Judas's bid for reclamation. He did not speak anymore as they headed through the gate of Hades, his final destination.

Judas Iscariot's thoughts ran wild as he traveled the rest of the way, past the Hades gate. The group followed closely behind the Messiah under the weight of mankind's sin, although at that moment they were still unaware of what he carried. Mephistopheles tried to make fun of him coming to Hades, thinking that because he died on the cross, the teacher would have to spend eternity under the dominion of Satan.

Death, who had been silent, became even more concerned. The look on his face caught the gatekeeper's attention. The gatekeeper looked back at Death as the latter too walked through showed concern about something. However, the gates closed as if on command and drew Mephistopheles' attention from Death momentarily. Again the gatekeeper was concerned about the automatic function of the gate.

"Who did that? was his stunned question to no one in particular. "I'm the gatekeeper and the only one other than Satan who can command the doors to be opened or closed!"

Still, Christ smiled but said nothing to the question.

"Let me ask you a question, Mephistopheles. Why did you leave your post today? Were you not to remain there constantly to allow in those who come here?"

Mephistopheles, with an embarrassed look, buried his face at the question. "I cannot tell him that I was ordered to be there for his death and lead him here!"

"Oh, but I already knew that answer, Meph. I already knew the answer!"

Death tried to respond to give indication as to why he was concerned but found himself unable to speak. He also wanted to tell them that Christ had opened and closed the gate but found that he could not speak. All the same, whatever has been bothering him about the Messiah had to wait. The triumph of the day was, here was the son of God coming to reside in the devil's den, as he so fondly referred to Hades. Furthermore, what he said about being in control—although it sounded far-fetched—could be true.

This has been too easy, he kept thinking. "Something about this whole episode smells of a trap, not of our setting." But as he wrestled with the barely conscious troubling thought, it continued to stay on the periphery of his consciousness. He and the group heard the far-off noise of laughter. Satan and the rest of the demons were celebrating.

The Messiah, not concerned about the obvious celebration that the devil was having, continued his measured trek down the path leading from the open gate. Iscariot followed behind with despair written all over his face. He began to feel the heat more intensely now. However, without realizing it, his body could not respond with the customary perspiration that normally accompanied such heat while he was alive.

"This body was so well made that while I was alive," Judas lamented. "I could count on it to produce perspiration to cool off, fight off the desert heat. Now, for some unknown reason, it is not reacting in its usual manner to the rising heat!"

The gatekeeper looked over at Judas and Etchers in amusement, temporarily distracted from what bothered him and conjured up a smile of gratification. However, Death was lost in thought, grappling with whatever was bothering him. This has been all too easy for the son of God to be here so meekly.

I need to speak to Satan immediately because something is wrong, Death thought. "Something about the way the Messiah is taking all this in. This is not right.

"I need a conference with Satan immediately, but how can I approach him? This is his moment of victory, and the sounds that are coming from the direction of his throne indicate that this may not be the right time to broach to him my concern. More than that, there are too many unanswered questions that need to be addressed! I guess that I will wait for a more appropriate time," Death mused.

The gatekeeper gave up trying to decipher what had so subtly crept into his mind lest he dampen a joyous occasion. I will eventually figure it out," he thought.

He seems to know where he is going, both Death and the gatekeeper thought of the teacher.

But Reality said nothing. As a matter of fact, from the time that the Messiah arrived at the place where they waited, Reality had become silent. To this, Judas commented to himself, "Reality knows what is going on. He knows that Death and Satan has lost but have not yet figured it out."

Reality kept looking furtively at his colleagues, Death and the gatekeeper, whimsical smile on his lips. "The entire Hades is going to break loose when they realize that they have just held the tiger by the tail."

The teacher looked over at Reality with that knowing smile, commenting to himself, "He has figured it out, and rightfully so. After all, he is Reality."

As Reality thought of the impending outcome, the Messiah did the unexpected. He stopped, turned under the weight of what he was carrying, looked at Reality, and said, "You are so right!"

The teacher then smiled, turned, and continued his trek. In that fleeting moment, Judas realized the truth.

"This man," the traitor murmured, "this Messiah was right all along, and I did not pay any attention! I was so caught up in my selfishness and materialism that it simply passed me by.

"Oh, Father God, what have I done?"

Christ, reading his mind, said, *"Now you know what you have done."* And the Lord kept on walking.

Darkness came no closer to the gates. He knew that it was not necessary anymore.

Adheres in Abraham's Bosom

In paradise, on the other side of the void, Adheres watched as Christ traveled down the path toward the gate with the small group preparing to enter. Adheres was paying attention not to his surroundings but at the party across the void which was about to enter Hades.

Etchers kept looking longingly in the direction that Adheres had gone, knowing that he would never see him again. The thought caused him to feel even more sorrowful and hopeless. "We were friends, companions for so long during our life," he cried. "Why didn't I follow him when we were on that cross?" As they neared the gates, desperation took over and encapsulated him.

Adheres, although now in Abraham's bosom, felt a kindred pain for the master, the Messiah. It was a kindred kind of pain and sorrow. But just as he was succumbing to it, he felt the Messiah in his mind saying, "Adheres, please, do not be concerned about me—this is what I came for! And as I have told you, this must be done so that you can have the joy and satisfaction of paradise. Besides, I'm enjoying every step I take in this direction, notwithstanding the pain, because I know the end of it! Yes, I do! So turn around and look—you will enjoy what you see."

From his vantage point on the balcony, Adheres glanced around just as Christ walked through the gates that seemed to open for him. He gasped and joyfully said the only thing that escaped his lips: "Paradise!"

I never thought that such simple words spoken by the Messiah would have produced such wonderful and bountiful happiness, he thought. "This is heaven—yes it is," Adheres exclaimed.

Suddenly, the voice of someone invaded the tranquility and pleasure that Adheres was bathed in. The voice said, "It is good to see you, my friend!"

Adheres turned to face the person behind the voice, which shocked him into reality. "The baptist!" he screamed.

"Yes, the Messiah will be along soon enough," John said as he perceived the thoughts of Adheres. "He must finish the function that the father assigned him, and that includes taking all our sins to Tartarus, the bottomless pit of Hades."

"Was it a long time coming?" asked Adheres.

"Yes! But for us time, is a tool that the father uses for the purpose of our doing the work which he has ordained us to do. You see, we—most of the population here—have been waiting for this moment for thousands of years. It was an agreement made by the father, Christ/Emmanuel, and the Holy Spirit, before Christ spoke everything into existence!

"Now, come on in. There are a lot of people waiting to greet and welcome you. Then you and I will tell the story of Christ and you on the cross."

"Christ?" Adheres asked. "The teacher spoke everything into existence? Is that what you said?"

"Yes!"

"This same Christ who has just entered into Hades?" Adheres pursued, "This same Christ who walked the country of Israel, Syria, Palestine, Samaria, and other places as a common man?

"Baptist, if I did not know that you told the truth, I would call you a liar! But I have known you to be truthful—at least it got you into the ultimate trouble with Herod and his sister in-law—so you would not lie to me now. Oh! How come the people who are still alive did not know this?"

"The answer is simple," explained the saint. "Their eyes and ears are closed to the truth of it all. They have their expectations, their pictures of how and who this Messiah would be. But nothing they saw of this lowly man is their depiction.

"You see, the people of Israel have been looking for a certain type of man to come and rescue them from the Romans, their present oppressors. But the father's plan was not outlined in that manner. A few believed that he was, even some of those who eventually had him crucified. But it had to be done unknown to them so that man can be saved.

"Adheres, his death is the payment for their sins. It is the cost of redemption from Satan and Death."

"His death on the cross was preordained?" Adheres queried. "He had to die and chose purposely to do it in that most gruesome manner? I died on a cross along with the Messiah! I felt pain like I have ever felt before! So why that method of death? Why not simply have someone kill him outright with a sword that would have been swifter? His death then would not have had the impact that it will from this point forward. It had to be dramatic and the worst way as dictated by the sin of man, to bring forth the effect that is necessary for some to believe."

John the Baptist continued and said, "We know. But something happened on that cross between you and the Messiah that caused you to be here! Words were spoken between the three of you, and we want to know! We, the residents of paradise, are curious to know what caused you to be here and your companion to be over there.

"Adheres, you are the first to be given the gift that you have received and the last to enter this place from the path of perdition. Many will want to speak to you about that now and later, when others walk the path that is now cleared by the Messiah to heaven.

"Allow me to explain: what happened to you on the cross that caused you to be here will be a conversation for many in the years to come.

"The teacher preached and taught many things while he was still alive; that will be misconstrued or believed as it was said.

"Those who misconstrue it will have thoughts that are contrary to the actual occurrence and your subsequent arrival here. Therefore, just as it has occurred and will be misconstrued by the living, the tendency can also be here among us who have been waiting for his return.

"So give, Adheres! What did he say to you and your companion on that cross?"

John had reached paradise some time previously and had continued the task that had been assigned to him by the teacher. He had to let those who had been here for so long waiting for the Messiah to come to know that he was on his way. The addition of Adheres to the paradise group was an addition that he welcomed in the preparation process.

Adheres had been the first to come to Abraham's bosom, having been saved through the death of Christ on the cross. This John believed and considered a selling tool of conviction for the residents of Abraham's bosom. John would tell them all to believe that the Messiah really had come and would be here in a very short while. Furthermore, Adheres would be the last to come to Abraham's bosom by way of the road of perdition. Adheres had a testimony that all the residents of paradise wanted to hear.

Adheres represented the long-awaited coming of the Messiah to Abraham's bosom. The Messiah had to come and preach to those who are here—as he had done to the living—so that they too would have a choice in accepting or denying him. It is a matter of choice for them even in death.

Jesus had said, "I'm the way, the truth, and the life. No one comes to the father except through me."[10]

Everyone in paradise knew this statement because John had already told them of this speech given by the teacher.

John addressed the residents. "Adheres' testimony of his salvation while on the cross will certainly be proof for those who are here waiting for Christ to come. And Adheres is here!"

While he spoke, many of the residents of Abraham's bosom came up, wanting to hear firsthand what transpired at Calvary on that fateful day. Thus, Adheres began to speak:

> I watched as the teacher groaned under the assault of death on that cross. I looked at him and knew that he did not do any of the things that Etchers and myself had done to be worthy of such a depraved death. Subsequently, when the people around started to mock him, I felt an injustice was being done to him.
>
> My companion Etchers, although on the verge of dying, joined with the crowd and began to mock him. It caught my attention. I reprimanded my associate for being such a dolt, knowing that the things we had done had brought us to this death. But from what I had seen and heard of this man, I could not accept that he had

done anything that remotely compared to what we had done. Therefore, I had a few words for Etcher.

I rebuked him, saying, "Do you not even fear God, seeing you are under the same condemnation? And we indeed justly, for we received the due reward of our deeds; but this man has done nothing wrong."[11]

I then said to Jesus, "Lord, remember me when you come into your kingdom."

And Jesus said to me, "Assuredly, I say to you, today you will be with me in paradise."[12]

I actually died before he did and began my journey to this place unknowingly.

What brought on the knowledge of the difference and subsequent assurance was when I caught up to Etchers and Judas Iscariot on the path to perdition."

They were both under the strain of some type of baggage, which seemed to grow out across the back of their shoulders. It seemed really heavy, but I had nothing like that! As a matter of fact, I found myself feeling rather weightless and bounded along as if propelled from behind.

It was then that I felt the thoughts of the teacher on my mind. I looked back to see him straining under a similar but much bigger baggage. It caused me to involuntarily ask the obvious question: why?

When I did, he somehow "mind linked" with me. He told me, "This is why I came—to die and take away the sins of mankind, pay the cost of their redemption—so that they can have life everlasting.

Today, as I look around, I do not see any of that baggage on any of you, so he must have your baggage also.

At that moment, everyone realized that they had indeed been stripped of the baggage they had carried—although they had been weightless to them.

"We really believed that the Messiah would come as the father had prophesied through the prophets, many of whom are here," said one resident.

As they realized the import of Adheres' words, they rejoiced simultaneously.

Adheres continued:

> Ladies and gentlemen, I know that the Messiah had said that to be saved, we must all be born again and baptized in the water. However, my death and rebirth was not that way unlike for the others because he is the Christ and has the power to save. That is what he came for, isn't it?
>
> And even to the last breath that the teacher breathed as a man, he continued to fulfill the father's will.
>
> Thus, I am here—saved—which means that the water portion is simply an outward rendition of what transpired in my life at Calvary.
>
> I am here because he has saved me from the fate of my companion Etcher. That is what counts!

And everyone in Abraham's bosom believed from that moment on!

John had come rushing to the gate, having been told by Christ while on the cross to expect Adheres.

The Messiah, John thought, thinks of everything. "Christ had covered all the bases in the redemption process of mankind. I'm sorry that so many of them will not listen and, subsequently, will end up on the other side like Adheres' friend Etchers. But this choice factor is the primary catalyst that they have—to choose whether they want to be here or over there.

"The testimony is here, and I have the pleasure of escorting him to the center to Abraham's bosom. Even as I think of it now, I know that the father is well pleased."

"Did you say something, John?" Adheres heard some of what John had said under his breath and thought that he was speaking to him.

"Oh no! I was simply thinking aloud!"

"So, am I a testimony? What does that mean?"

"It means that you are the confirmation that Christ sent ahead to let these who have been waiting for him that he is on his way! Furthermore, you did an excellent job of recalling to give the final confirmation to the residents of paradise."

Abraham had come up and heard all that Adheres had to say. So too did Adam and Eve, as well as Sarah, Abraham's wife. Thus, they all stood waiting with arms wide open to welcome him. Abraham hugged him and said, "My child, my descendant!"

Abraham shouted with glee and hugged him. John watched as Abraham embraced Adheres with a kiss on both cheeks. Adheres' body wracked with the emotion of joy that flooded his soul and couldn't keep it in.

"I'm here," Adheres exploded.

Abraham held him even closer, knowing how close he came to being on the other side with his previous companion Etchers.

"That is the wonder of the Messiah, Adheres!" Abraham said. "Even in Death's throws, he still does as the father asked him to do. We all watched as he fought to save Judas and prayed that Judas would hear his voice. But he was smothered by those whom the devil sent so that the Messiah's voice couldn't be clearly heard. Now, it is too late for him!

"I know that John will want to speak to you very soon, in preparation of the Messiah's appearance," said Abraham.

"You mean that he will come here?"

"I saw him go into the gates of the Hades with that heavy load! And the way that he was walking—purposely and measured—indicates that whatever it is that he was carrying was really very burdensome.

"Adheres, he was carrying the sins of yours, mine, and all others' who have died and those who will eventually die. Those are the sins of all who believed that he would come—and he has come. And they are a lot because they have accumulated since Adam and Eve sinned."

"Adam and Eve? Do you mean that they are here? I want to see them," said Adheres!

"Hold on!" said Abraham. "Remember the Messiah gave you a reprieve. Just as he forgave you, you also must forgive them!"

"You are absolutely right, Father Abraham. After all, the things that I have done while in my physical flesh were atrocious, but here I find myself, because of the few words that he spoke to me. I cannot wait to thank him."

"Now that you have realized that, I will introduce you to Adam," Abraham told Adheres. "I must tell you, of all the people who have been here, he has not been given very much opportunity to forget that he was primarily responsible for their demise. So please be forgiving."

"Father Abraham, I thank you for showing me this."

Adam was hesitant, having gone through a lot of questions as to why he ate the apple. He had been hurting, but he tried to be happy. He came over and looked at Adheres.

"Hello there!" said the first man ever. "Welcome to paradise. I'm glad that you made it. "You know, I watched as the Messiah was placed on that cross, alongside you and Etchers. I was pained and, at the same time, relieved that the promise of the father came to pass.

"Welcome, Adheres. I am glad that you have made it even in the last seconds of your life. It is a reprieve that all of us here at Abraham's bosom cherish—my wife and I more than any other."

They hugged for a long time. Adheres responded with the most wonderful thing at that moment, which made Adam feel better.

"You know, Adam," Adheres began, "I'm very glad to have got here by the skin of my teeth. I'm no better than any other person; therefore, I should not try to find fault or blame anyone for my life, what caused it. Least of all, I should not blame you or Eve. Simply put, the devil outsmarted you and many who followed. And before you, he outsmarted a third of the angels of heaven. So ease up on yourself. You were still innocent when it occurred.

"The devil chose his time for persuading you and Eve—when he thought that you were most vulnerable. Which, I might add, may have been the only thing that he did. More important, when the Messiah walked through those gates, the inhabitants of Hades were very uncertain about what would happen."

Adam bowed his head in recognition of the compliment that Adheres paid him, although it was only a fleeting thing. However, Adheres continued, "When the Messiah comes, he will also let you know that he has forgiven you and has made everything right. So cheer up. He will be here!"

"Thank you, Adheres! I needed that reminder!" said Adam.

John approached the group, having waited until the introductions were completed and both persons were well met. The baptist recognized the need for Adam to feel some of the weight of guilt being lifted off him. John somehow knew that Adheres would say the right thing.

Obviously, John was correct because Adam was smiling, something that was rarely seen. After all, Adam had been carrying a weight that no one would have to carry. But pretty soon, it would be all over! Everything will be set right and back on tract!

As John approached, Abraham looked in his direction and beamed with laughter and joy. "John, here you are! Knowing you, I'm sure that you want to get started preparing everyone for the Messiah's arrival. I also know that you want Adheres to testify to everyone. I anticipate an excellent outcome."

"Thank you, Father Abraham!" John chimed back. But I believe that it is already done! Take a look at the faces of everyone! Those who were not at the testimony given to you have already heard it from others, and that is the key. They believe! And because they believe, they are now free to await the presence of Messiah among them! Hallelujah!"

John's booming voice echoed across paradise as he announced the arrival of Adheres. "Brethren, we have our first blood-bought guest with us!" he shouted.

A shout of joy unlike what transpired over in Hades rang out.

"Welcome," was the resounding response that was filled with real joy! "It is good to have you among us."

One of the prophets spoke up. He had extricated himself from the gathering crowd to shake Adheres' hand. "Do you know that you are the first to be saved by the blood of the Messiah? You are the true example of what he came to achieve, and that gives us reason to be happy. We watched the episode at Calvary unfold. Welcome!"

"I thank you for that compliment . . . but . . . who . . . are you?"

"Oh, I'm sorry. My name is Jeremiah!"

"I have heard of you! When I was a child growing up in my parents' home, they told me of you!" Adheres responded. "Did you happen to know where they are now?"

"They will be along shortly," Jeremiah said. "But tell us, what does it feel like to have all your sins washed away by his blood?"

"Oh, like a feather that has been let loose from the wings of an eagle in flight—real light!"

Laughter rang throughout the gathering after Adheres made that comment. None of them had experienced that type of feeling before. They now did and knew exactly what he meant. It was a good feeling, and they were waiting impatiently to know more.

The only thing that they did not experience was the joy that came from being saved from sin by the blood of the chosen lamb of God. Jesus was the one that the father had promised, and the residents could not wait to see him in person.

"My friends, if I understand it correctly, the blood of the Messiah also washed your sins away! Therefore, you too are cleansed and made whole! You are no longer carrying the sack that was attached to you, isn't that correct?"

"Yes!"

"You are correct; come to think of it!" Abraham said. "I imagine that we do not have to wait to have that same experience as soon as the Messiah is finished over there! We already have, from the time that we believed you and his forerunner John!

"We will all be able to look at the Messiah in person, see the nail prints in his hands and feet, the spear-pierced wound in his side, and know that it was all for us." Meanwhile, John felt some of his burdens lifting because in his own way, Adheres was doing exactly what he, John, wanted—to convince those who were there that Messiah was coming soon! The joy of it all, the expectation, of the coming Messiah just made John so ecstatic that he couldn't hold it in. "Yes! This is wonderful!" he said. "And to think that the father chose me to proclaim his coming! Satan thought that he has won, but he is in for the surprise of his life!"

And so everyone in Abraham's bosom joined in celebration, anticipating the Messiah's coming. Simultaneously they all went to look over the railing, to the void that separated both places of Hades. Christ was just about to step into the entrance to Tartarus.

Amadden

Abraham was the happiest of all, happier than even Adam, who became animated at knowing that his mistake was about to be completely wiped out. His mistake was being righted even as they gathered at the railing and around Adheres.

I guess that I can understand his problem, said John to himself. He did not realize that Abraham was looking at him, and the latter's response caught him off guard.

"Yes, John! It is not easy to shake the fact that every person who is now occupying the other side is there because of his lack of responsibility. In a way, he was supposed to have done differently, but . . . the Messiah is going to have to work on him more than any other person who now resides over here. So let us hug and cheer him up!"

In the pit in Tartarus, an unequaled scream rose up—crescendo upon crescendo—to the residents of Hades, drowning out their cries. They too had heard Gabriel's trumpet and recognized it. Never before had they felt pain emanate from it as it did in those moments. Their pain surpassed that which they had been forced to live with for so long. One demon in particular jumped up, and he too froze. He froze from the pain as well as from hearing that sound in Tartarus.

"What is going on?"

"Did Gabriel decide to join us?"

"And did the father allow him to bring his trumpet with him when he did not allow Lucifer to do so?"

"No! Something is wrong!"

"Something is not right here!"

"The father would not have allowed that trumpet to leave heaven to come here!"

"He did not do it when he threw out Lucifer, and he would not do it now!"

"What did Lucifer do this time?"

"It must be because of something that idiot has done, that pompous fool."

"He does not know when to leave well alone! And that will be his undoing eventually."

Simultaneously he felt the pull of someone who was bound for his domain.

"Oh?"

"No!"

"It cannot be Gabriel coming here, it must some other angel or human who have been evil beyond what the father can stand!"

And so, Amadden began a journey upward from the bottom of the pit. Meanwhile, in Hades Satan and his band of merrymakers prepared to meet Christ at the door to test him about being there in Tartarus and to check on the piece of luggage that he brought with him. It was at that moment of expectation that Gabriel's trumpet sounded, catching all the residents of Hades and Tartarus off guard.

Christ knew what was ahead of him. He knew that torment and ridicule waited for him as he strolled down through Hades to Tartarus.

Satan and his cohorts will be there to welcome me, he thought. "And they will gourd me, test me, and try to torment me more. It is expected as a part of the price that I must pay for man's redemption."

And so Christ, with a set face, continued his journey as if he were familiar with the place. Nothing that they said deterred him from his set path. It made the gatekeeper, who had left his customary post on this auspicious occasion, introspective about the whole thing.

Nothing in his demeanor is right for this place, Mephistopheles mused.

The red and eeriness of night now enclosed the realm of Hades. Death followed the procession past the gate, something that he rarely did. It was the first night of the Messiah in hell. There was always someone dying, which drew Death's attention from the gates. But today he felt the urge to come in and visit for a while.

What will transpire here tonight, Death thought, will be very interesting, and I want to be here for it. And so as Death strode down the avenue of Hades, his eyes searched for Satan and rested on him. "Hmm! There is something bothering him; I can feel it. He is trying to mask it, but that cannot be done. I can sense it. It must be the blowing of that trumpet. Thinking about it caused him momentary pain. Hmm?"

The other residents of Hades gathered behind the Messiah. There were two contingents of them. There were those who were hopeful, knowing who he was. They hoped to be forgiven and given the opportunity to leave Hades. They thought that they had suffered enough and that the father would now allow them to leave.

Even Cain, who had killed his brother Abel, was there. He remembered the conversation that he had with the father on that fateful day. Cain wondered if he would now have the chance to be forgiven and allowed to leave this godforsaken place. The look from the Messiah's eyes told him no, and he wilted. All momentary hope was dragged from him in that fleeting moment.

Does the father not forgive? Cain asked himself.

Jesus, reading Cain's mind, beamed back at him. "You know better. You were given the opportunity to ask his forgiveness, but you were arrogant. You asked him if he thought that you were your brother's keeper!"

Cain bowed his head in hopelessness.

The other contingent was composed of those who knew that there was no hope for them. Viewing the scene and knowing the truth, they knew that they had already blown any opportunity to be redeemed. These ones decided to turn their hopelessness of redemption into hopefulness that Christ would be staying with them for all eternity, because it would then validate their actions during their life. However, in their minds rang the words "Not so, you had your chances. I will not be staying here with you."

These hopeless souls too looked on with frustration as the words of condemnation coursed through their tormented minds.

> "Yes! This is forever for you. Now you see me, but in
> a little while, you will not. Ha!"

They replied to the onslaught of words that filled their mind, causing others to look at them as they made the statement. Most thought that they were actually laughing at the Messiah for being there.

"Satan will have something to say about that!"

To wit, Satan looked at them, and then at Christ. Hmm, what is going on here, he thought to himself.

At that moment, the teacher looked at Satan with eyes that penetrated to the core of the latter's being. Again, something caused Satan to ponder.

"Did I do something wrong? Or is there something that have I left undone?"

Death was pensive, not saying much, except to acknowledge Satan, who had left his throne room to come and greet the Messiah. Reality, on the other hand, seemed to be the only one who knew what was going on, but he was not saying anything. It was as if he had received orders that he had to carry out.

Oh boy, mused Reality, all hell will be in an uproar when they find out why and what he is here for. There will be a lot of sorry faces, as well as disappointment. They have no clue! The Messiah is here as was foretold. But not to save the residents of Hades—only to deliver his baggage and diminish the power of Death and Satan. I feel it in my bones, and I will do my best not to be around Satan when that is made clear to him."

And so the procession continued down the path that had been cleared for the group. The residents of hell lined up on both sides of the entering party.

The Messiah trudged on, not turning to the right or left. He felt the mind touch of Amadden but did not let on that he did. He knew that there was anger, frustration, and a pensiveness in the mind link. Amadden wanted to know why he was there so soon but received no response.

Ahead was a rather dark and more eerie area, darker than the other red-lit areas where the blaze from the fire danced, as if hand in hand with the pervading darkness. To this area, Christ continued his march. Then it simultaneously dawned on Death and Satan that Christ was heading for Tartarus, that part of Hades where the most hideous and dangerous of the demons were chained.

"Is he going to unshackle them?" Death and Satan asked. They were coetaneous and looked at each other. The question that they raised caused the eyebrows of the other demons to look with consternation at Death and Satan.

"Tartarus? That means that any minute now Amadden will poke his head over the top of that pit!"

The mere thought of Amadden caused them to look furtively at the entrance, at the Christ, and at Satan, as if looking for some directive from either of them. But none was forthcoming.

They were scared! Not of Death, and definitely not of Satan, because with these demons loose, more havoc would be loose on the earth and in Hades. More important, the demons obviously knew about them. Some obviously had firsthand knowledge of those who were chained in the bottomless pit. Still, as the Messiah glanced at Satan, he knew that this devil was indeed scared of Amadden.

The demons of Tartarus were not just a menace to humans but to demons as well. These were the most vicious and atrocious of all the demons, Death and the gatekeeper included. On the other hand, Satan envisioned a reign of terror unlike any that humanity had ever experienced. Yet Christ moved closer and closer to Tartarus, not paying any attention to those who thought that he had lost.

Judas, following behind and to the side with Etchers, was looking for a place where he thought that he could be most comfortable, when the teacher invaded his mind and said, "Don't even think of it! You belong with me. Where I go, you go too!"

Judas did not know how to take the comment but felt that he might have won some kind of reprieve from him.

"No, Judas," Jesus continued. "You have not won a reprieve; you have won the honor of being one of the worst evil that God allowed to live. You sold out His only begotten son for thirty pieces of silver. Now your reward is at hand."

Judas groaned and wept! "Teacher, if I had not done this thing, someone else would have! Otherwise, you would not be here with the sins of man, accomplishing the father's will!"

"That is true, Judas. But it didn't have to be you. The chief priests and the Pharisees would have done it themselves, and you would not be here now. However, your greed for material wealth overrode your desire to be saved from eternal damnation of the worst kind. Follow along."

Judas groaned more heavily because he saw how the demons and other residents of Hades reacted when they realized where he and the Messiah were going: Tartarus.

Etchers looked on, perplexed. "Judas, why are you following him? Do you want to go to Tartarus with him? Aren't you scared of that place? Look at how these people are reacting. They are cowering, which means that to them it is not a place they would want to be in. It must be really bad there!"

"Etchers, I do not have a choice," Judas answered. "It is as if the teacher has a rope around my neck, and I cannot pull against it. I must go there because of what I have done."

"Yes! It is a little late for either of us to recognize our misdeeds, isn't it?"

Judas shrugged his shoulder under the weight of his sins, and that too brought much pain. Etchers, although he was hurting now more than ever, felt a certain sorrow for this man who walked the distance to Hades with him. No sooner had Etchers started reflecting on the fate of Judas than he was yanked around by a demon and placed alongside the road to Tartarus with instructions not to move.

"Here you will stay until you are told to move, and that can be for a long time," the demon said.

Etchers then felt more pain and looked down to see a worm borough into his instep. He cried out at the pain. Everyone looked around at him, and then realized that he was a newcomer.

The journey to Tartarus seemed to take forever as Christ, burdened with the sins of the world, drew closer. The package on his back and shoulders contained every sin and curse of the law that had been placed on mankind through Adam's sin. Even Adam and Eve's sins and curses were riding on his back.

And as Christ walked and thought of it, he reflected that he had to circumvent or undo what Adam and Eve did. Indeed, he had become the "second Adam."

Suddenly, there was a hush, one unlike any that had ever permeated Hades. A name was called, one that was feared even in this godforsaken place.

"Amadden! Amadden!"

The name escaped from Death's mouth rather involuntarily and caused the gatekeeper to spin around, half expecting the Amadden personage to be standing there. His face was pale, as something about that name affected him.

"Who said that? Why does anyone want to call that name without a reason?"

"Oops, sorry. It just came out, and I do not even know why!" said Death.

There was something about that name that shook Death and the gatekeeper.

"Death, this is not the time to be funny!"

"Oh, I was not trying to be funny. I do not know why I said his name."

Judas heard the name, and for no reason, his reaction caused grave alarm to Etchers, who stood rooted where he was planted!

"Who is this Amadden? Etchers called to Judas. Do you know him? And why is everyone reacting like this?"

Judas had also become pale and obviously distraught.

"Judas, what is going on? Why are you looking like you ate something sour? Do you know this Amadden?" Etchers called after Judas a second time.

"No!" the former disciple finally replied. "It is the first time that I heard of him. I have never been told of him."

Death would not talk to the gatekeeper, and the latter became the most silent and furtive person in the group heading through Hades and toward Tartarus, the final destination of Jesus and Judas.

Reality was the first to give an explanation, as Judas's eyes riveted to him. As he was giving his explanation, Judas too began to mouth the words without realizing or knowing why.

"Amadden is the person who guards the most awful of places in Hades—the place called Tartarus," Reality said. "In this dungeon, this pit, the most evil of all is sent there until Christ . . . comes . . . back."

"Huh? Why did I say that?" Judas asked. "I do not know this demon, so why should be I struck by his name and seem to know so much about him?" Judas said.

"He is waiting for you!"

Judas jumped involuntarily as the words penetrated his mind. "Huh? Who? What? Teacher, did you say that?" Judas asked.

It was not said verbally but through the mind link that Christ had been using all along.

"Yes, I did!"

"Which of you is heading for Tartarus," said Death, sensing something? It is only when the worst of all humans comes here that we feel and hear his name, so which one of you is going down to Tartarus?"

Again the effect of the name on the gatekeeper became visible again. "Amadden is reaching out to someone here, and I need to know which of you is the one to whom he is reaching out! Or is it him—the so-called son of God?"

"Why? Why do you want to know?" asked Judas?

"Amadden cannot go far from Tartarus, but he can draw people to him," Mephistopheles explained. "Even demons have fallen prey to him over the years. So he is not someone that we like to be around with. He has a strength of mind that reaches beyond the gates of Hades. No one is ever really safe around him."

Suddenly, along with the long silence that had overcome Hades, the residents who had lined up on both sides of the path started edging away from the party. The residents did not want to be near the traveling party because they had the idea that one or more in this group attracted the attention of this most feared demon.

Judas looked at the Messiah, and then at Mephistopheles, who looked back at him.

"Do you think that maybe you are the one who is going to this place, this Tartarus, Judas?" the gatekeeper asked.

Judas jerked upright at the comment and caused Mephistopheles to think that maybe he was the one that Amadden was reaching out for. Judas became silent suddenly and looked again at the Messiah. Iscariot's thoughts were now racing as if on a chariot pulled by four horses going around a steep corner.

"Yes, Judas, it is you! Answer him! It is you who will be going down there!" The Messiah had touched Judas's mind. No one knew that the conversation occurred until Judas screamed at the top of his lungs causing everyone to simultaneously look at him, except for the Messiah who continued his purposeful walk.

"No! . . . No! Messiah! Have mercy on me!"

"As I have told you, it is too late for you or any other person who has crossed those gates that we left behind!"

Death edged away from Judas, as did Mephistopheles. Over in the shadows, Reality and Confusion were scared and momentarily witless.

"It does not matter which of them Amadden calls out to; I do not want to be near them," said Reality.

"That can be a very dangerous encounter, particularly if Amadden is reaching this far out from Tartarus," Confusion commented. "Whoever it is must have done something really awful, and it could be this Judas!"

"Of course, he did," responded Reality to Confusion's assessment. "He sold out his mentor, teacher, and Messiah, if the information on him is correct."

The only thing that seemed to stop Judas from running to this unseen personage with such powerful mind touch was his burden of sin, his stomach literally trailing him, and the Messiah's overriding mental strength.

"Amadden, you will do nothing until I tell you to. He will enter Tartarus with me. I will want to place him where he will remember for all eternity that he sold me out to the chief priest and his hirelings. So leave him alone for now and back off."

The realm of Hades suddenly rocked with a wail like that which they had heard when Gabriel blew his horn. Amadden wailed because he was touched by the Messiah's mind, and it was painful to him. Yet he had not yet crested the opening of Tartarus to show his face.

"Messiah," Amadden called out mentally, "why are you coming here? It is not yet time to punish us!

"Lucifer, what have you done this time? What evil have you done, causing the Messiah to come here already?"

Satan was very shaken by Amadden's question in his mind. The devil had always tried to avoid this demon; any contact with him can be distressing. Thus, Satan had always wondered if he was really in charge of this demon. "Maybe I should have left him in heaven so that the father can deal with him himself. He is unruly and uneasy to be around with. I can never know what he is thinking." Satan was really shook up and commented to no one in particular, "Did we make a mistake in killing this Messiah?"

Amadden's head poked over the ridge of the hole, and all eyes in Hades focused on him and the demons that had preceded him through the opening. These demons were chained together to form a procession before him. He repeated the question that he had mind linked to Satan. "What have you done this time? What evil have you done, causing the Messiah to come here already?"

Satan's face for the first time turned into an ash grey. This was not anger but fear. As the devil tried to bolster himself in this demon's presence, he thought, here we go again. "Am I really in charge here, or is this demon the one who is really in charge?"

Amadden heard the comment of Christ's crucifixion from someone on the side, and he looked at Satan. "Is that what you did? Did you not know the scriptures? Did you not know that you did exactly what he and the father wanted?"

After Amadden made the remark, he became silent and glum. A changed look took place in his demeanor that seemed to rob him of the expected joy of having another resident in Tartarus. Satan looked blankly at the demon, although staying some distance away, and wondered, What is it that he knows that I do not know?

Meanwhile, the Messiah was making his way to the completion of the destiny that he had chosen.

"I'm surely glad that I froze Amadden's mouth before he could say more, giving Satan more information than he needed at this time. Amazingly, these demons are afraid of Amadden, who is simply a puppet, a shadow of the real power—the father.

"Because he is able to guard Tartarus and keep those who are chained there from escaping, everyone is scared of him, even Judas. Look how he is quivering, not looking forward to this destiny that he chose."

And these thoughts filled Messiah's mind as he trudged on with timely precision.

Meanwhile, a scene was unfolding over in Abraham's bosom while Christ was getting closer to Tartarus. The residents were becoming more aware of a certain joy and uplifting that they had not witnessed before. Adam, who was the first to notice it, became jovial, jubilant, and excited.

Why do I feel this way? the first man asked himself. "I have not had such a feeling since before I ate that fruit from Eve. What is happening?"

Simultaneously, others began acting more free, more jovial than before. John was the first to identify the cause. "Don't you see?" he said. "The sins that have been with you while you waited for the Messiah, their hold is constantly being removed from you the closer he gets to Tartarus. You are being freed of the burden of sins that have been with you, although you did not know it!"

The shout that went up at that revelation reverberated all the way to Hades.

And the Messiah smiled! "They know! They now know!"

Judas, who had been following behind while cowering from Amadden, also heard the joyous shout and reflected that he would never enjoy that environment. He let out a shout of pain, unlike any he had previously felt. Gone was the opportunity, as was hope, well as forgiveness. "I am now lost forever!"

Then Christ felt a twinge of sorrow but knew that he could not now allow this to overtake him. Satan and his cohorts would have a field day if I was to now forgive this man, Christ thought. This is the price that I must pay, he kept muttering to himself, and it is well worth it. "Yes, mankind is worth it, and the joy that is coming from over yonder is confirmation of it. If even a remnant is saved, it is truly worth it. The simple love that some of them will show the father after this is finished will be payment enough to Jahveh. "For this reason, I will endure this tirade and the punishment that await me. For as many as are of the works of the law are under the curse. For it is written, "Cursed is everyone who does not continue in all things which are written in the book of the law to do them."

And so the journey to Tartarus drew on with precision. Christ's measured steps told the story of the burden that was on his back and shoulders, and Judas following behind. And he thought, "This is nothing compared to what I just went through on that cursed cross. No, not Junior, but what he had to become to accommodate this war between Death, Satan, and myself. And I can see that they still do not have a clue as to what has and will happen.

"However, they will, but it will be too late for them to do anything, not that they can anyway. My father has given me the authority to walk into and out of this place with no one touching me.

"I have done as the father asked, and this then is my protection. I have done his will! Yes, it does not matter—I have resigned myself to doing the father's will, and I will be victorious! I will do this three nights and three days, living on the fact that I and mankind will be rid of this evil, if they utilize the grace that my father gave me. It is not the law anymore but grace, abundant grace for all who believe that I came to die for them at the request of the father!"

Then Christ said to Judas, "Judas, are you following me?"

"Yes . . . Messiah, I am . . . following you."

"Now you recognize me as the Messiah when it is too late for you. I gave you so many opportunities to claim your rightful position with me instead, but you claim this position that you now inherit.

"And yes, Judas, you will be punished more than any human who comes to this place because you gave away eternal life for a temporary gratification that you could not even enjoy!

"For what profit is it to a man if he gains the whole world and loses his own soul?[13] Amadden is waiting for you to bind you in that bottomless pit of Tartarus, where you will spend eternity. What pity? What loss?"

Judas wanted to lash out at anything for his stupidity and looked at the teacher's back as the thought ran through his mind.

"Judas, do not make a sad situation any worse for you!"

"Huh?"

"You heard me well. Do not make a sad situation any worse for you!"

From that moment on, Judas would not allow his mind to drift in that direction. He knew when he was beaten. Still, communicating with the Messiah eased his burden somewhat.

"What will happen with this Amadden, Teacher? What will he do to me? And why are Death, the gatekeeper, and these others so scared of him? Why do I feel pure, unadulterated dread, fear when I hear that name?"

"Because," Jesus responded, "it was designed that way as part of your punishment, and for any other who is destined for that place."

"Teacher, how is it that you did not come as the son of God?"

"I came as the son of God, Judas, but you, like the rest of the high priests, the Pharisees, and the Sanhedrin, was looking for someone dressed in kingly garments and ready to supernaturally throw the Romans out and place them in the driver's seat.

"Obviously, you all did not read the books of prophesy from the prophets of old. Or in reading them, you interpreted them the way that you wanted them to be. However, your interpretation or theirs changes nothing.

"So many of them prophesied my coming, and the manner it would happen, but very few of Israel paid any attention to the details. To think that you had the Messiah, the perfect lamb, that was talked about by Isaiah and many others. Still, you did not believe!

"Judas, unlike many of the Jews, you were given firsthand information of me and from me because I did not want you to come here. But you did not take advantage of it, even after hearing me speak so often. Judas, I knew who you were when I chose you to join me! I did not want you to come here; therefore, I hoped that being with me would change you heart. But it didn't, so here we are. And here you are to remain for all eternity. Amadden is really waiting to get his hands on you!"

"Oh! Teacher! Messiah! Truly, I'm sorry, about all this and do need your forgiveness. You once told Simon Peter to forgive seventy times seven! So why do you not forgive me?"

"Judas you had a lifetime to forgive and receive forgiveness, as I have forgiven those who have trespassed against me. You had that opportunity, and you proved it by reiterating what I said to Peter. Now it is time for you to face the music of Reality. Come along."

They had not yet come in sight of Amadden, but his influence ranged all the way to them. Still, the nearer the group came to him, the stronger was his mind pull on Judas Iscariot. Christ's consolation came as he measured his steps to the precipice of darkness and Amadden.

Christ thought of the end of it all and his subsequent return home via paradise—Abraham's bosom. These were incentive enough to keep him moving in the direction of the ultimate pain and suffering that he was asked to pay for man's redemption. But more important and primary was getting rid of this load of refuse that he must deposit in this bottomless pit. Everyone could feel the tension that was building here in this godforsaken place.

I can feel Amadden's anxiety as I get nearer to him, Christ thought. "He does not know how to act toward me. But more important, he is also antagonizing Lucifer even as I speak. Satan may think that he has won, but wait until I unload this garbage, do my stint in Tartarus, and then knock on his doors. Boy, I cannot wait to see the look on his and Death's face at that moment. That is incentive enough for me!"

And so the time dragged on, and the evening dragged on.

They will know then that the father's word does not fail, that I have not failed, while they have lost, Christ assured himself. "Oh, that is the moment of my triumph—when I relieve them of the keys of Death and Hell. Patience Jesus." He said this to encourage himself as he walked toward his prescribed destinations.

Whenever he felt like unloading his burden right there at the devil's feet, he simply looked past Hades to Abraham's bosom to know that he had won!

"No!" he said to himself. "Not my will but my father's, who sent me to accomplish this task. I will not be deterred now, not for all of the so-called riches and wealth that this idiot tried to buy me with. And the stupidity of it all is that he thinks that it is his. Well, we will see who laughs last! We will see who the ultimate victor is!

"Come along, Iscariot. Do not tarry! I have a job to complete to the glory of the father!"

Tartarus drew closer, Amadden, nearer. With each step, the Messiah realized the price could not have been paid by any other person or spirit. With that thought in his mind, Christ's joy and sorrow were simultaneous. He thought of the impending trauma that he must undergo at the cost of mankind, and in the proximity of those who are trapped at the bottom of Tartarus.

But it is all for a worthy cause, the Messiah consoled himself. "Reality is very courageous, I must say, because he seems to be keeping steps with me. He is the only one who seems to know what is going to happen in this godless place. But let's see how close he will come to Amadden; every one of these inhabitants is dreadfully afraid of this demon."

Then Christ did everything in his power as a human spirit to encourage himself as he neared the most dangerous part of his journey. "It is one thing for Amadden to recognize me as the Messiah; but as a human, I am not sure what his reaction will be."

And so he continued this self conversation to stay himself on the path which he had chosen as the Christ!

"This is my task to which I had committed myself long before I spoke the world into existence. I knew that this would happen and have prepared for it. So now is the moment of truth."

While Jesus walked toward the edge of Tartarus and toward destiny, someone pushed at the weight he carried and caused him to stagger. Yet he smiled and continued. A curious resident—a demon, and one so bold—reached out and touched the load of Christ and screamed at the top of his lungs. Touching the baggage cost the demon more than he had bargained for. The pain was excruciating, and this made the Messiah smile.

"Hmm! If Satan only knew. If he could get past the block that I have placed on him and his cohorts, they would think differently of this situation."

Christ too was in constant agony, and the holes in his hands, feet, and his left side did not help his situation much. Still, he trudged on. To those who looked on, he did it effortlessly.

I will do this! I will do this! he said to himself.

Outside the gates of Hades, Darkness waited patiently! He knew that his job was not yet done, but did not know why he knew it! He waited patiently!

The Messiah saw Amadden, even as the latter seemed to recognize him also. Amadden's reaction was genuine—he seemed to want to crawl back over the edge of the pit to escape the Messiah's penetrating gaze.

Even here, he commands a lot of respect, thought Amadden. "I wonder how this will play out! Will I be placed down there with my so-called compatriots? Will I be allowed to develop a meaningful relationship with him? Or maybe now I will receive some understanding. That would beat standing here and disallowing the residents from below to become acquainted with this upper part of perdition. Chained as they are, I still do not trust them as far as I can spit! It would be great to see the look on his face if one or two of them were to emerge and confront him. I know that they hold a lot of animosity toward him for their dilemma.

Satan and Amadden stood near the entrance of Tartarus. Satan was standing out of Amadden's reach. Amadden had a reputation with the lesser demons that Satan did not want to experience. Thus, for that reason, Satan didn't allow the distance between both of them to become any nearer. Those who had preceded Amadden out of the pit were the demons who had fallen prey to his dominance.

The bully is afraid of one of his underlings, would you believe that? the teacher thought of Lucifer. "He is so vulnerable, and he does not even know it! I should let Amadden go for a second and see what this evil one, Satan, would do. It would be interesting." But Christ thought better of it. "Not my will but my father's will be done."

The minor demons were all lined up leading to the mouth of Tartarus, all trying to see what would happen and at the same time, scoring points with their master, Satan. Subsequently, they were jostling and pushing at the load that the Christ carried. Their efforts were rewarded with intense pain, deterring any other who thought of following suit. On the other hand, Christ had come too far to be deterred by some underling demon who sought to get his master's attention by being idiotic.

The march continued. It was still the evening of the first day. Two more nights and two days were left in this godforsaken place, and no one was more conscious of it than Christ was.

"My respite is awaiting me on the next day in Abraham's bosom, and I can think of no better place to spend it except at my father's right hand. Everything in due time, he found himself thinking. "He who laughs last has the best laugh."

And Christ Jesus intended to have the last laugh.

The evening dragged on as Jesus moved toward Tartarus, Amadden with Judas Iscariot trailing behind him, now hiding more behind him than before. Jesus recognized Amadden as the one who would be in charge of him from the time that he entered the pit. Christ smiled wistfully as he thought of what would occur, particularly with Iscariot in Amadden's hands.

I'm sorry for you Judas, he said to himself.

Judas seeming to understand what the teacher was thinking. Iscariot likewise said to the master, "I am sorry that I did not listen to you before, Teacher."

Time seemed to stand still for Christ in Hades as he walked the path that eventually became a gauntlet. Demons were pushing and mocking and, at the same time, feeding off the emotions of those who had already dared to be obnoxious. However, none would dare to push the bundle that Christ had across his shoulders. They had learned the hard way that whatever he had on his back caused a multitude of pains.

Now the agony on the cross seems light in comparison to the punishment that the demons were intent on meting out to Christ without touching the baggage on his back. Yet he trudged on, seemingly oblivious to what was happening to him, with Judas following meekly behind. He consoled himself by comparing each act of molestation committed by his demon-antagonists with what each soldier meted out to him in Pilot's praetorium. Not as much but more than the soldiers did. Yes, definitely worse, not as bad.

He continued the process of comparison, and it served as a distraction for him as he fought against the consuming pain in his body. If the devil only picked up on this, had any knowledge that he was hurting, "I am sure that he would have the pleasure of encouraging more demons to join in the fray. However, I will not give them that pleasure. They will not know yet how I feel."

Some of the human residents, while in their pain and agony, looked with hope at the scene of the Messiah-Christ in their midst, having recognized him immediately. "Messiah! Messiah! Messiah!"

The human residents in their pain and agony looked at him as their savior, to take them out of the hell in which they found themselves. One resident asked an alarming and intriguing question, "How did we come to that conclusion that he is the Messiah? The fact that I recognize him as the Messiah despite not having seen or spoken to him before is mind-boggling."

The Messiah then felt the worst pain that he had ever experienced since taking on the form of man. It was the pain in his heart, knowing that he could do nothing for these people, whose hopes for salvation were aroused at the sight of him. The demon residents were oblivious to the environment because they felt no pain.

Only when one of the demons touched Christ's package did they feel pain—something new to them. Thus, they mocked the humans for their cries of pain and anguish and reached out to the Messiah in expectation of redemption, one that would never come. The Messiah turned as the ones who were nearest to him cried out his name, although they have never seen him before.

"Salvation, Messiah! Salvation, please!"

The pain of the statement poured out into his heart and mind with increasing voracity, unlike any that he had felt before. It seemed that the closer the Messiah got to them, the more pain that he and they felt.

"Save us, Teacher. Save us from this damnation! You came to save us, so here we are! Please take me away from here."

The Messiah's lungs were filled with emotion ready to come forth, but he fought against it. "I must get to Tartarus quickly. I do not know how long I can bear this agony of hopelessness that they are suffering. The pain is unlike any other pain! I, who is hope myself, am suffering this pain because I cannot offer hope!"

Meanwhile, Judas who was following closely, found that the pain was even more excruciating to him. The pain became a constant reminder of what he chose while in life. Judas wept!

Pontius Pilate's praetorium, where soldiers beat and mocked Christ, pulling at his beard and spitting on him, now seemed far away. All that seems so inconsequential now, Jesus thought.

The pain—spiritual, mental, and physical—was really telling on Jesus, as if this purposeful attack was designed to stop him from entering Tartarus. "Father, I will complete this mission, if for no other reason than to reap vengeance on Satan for all that he has caused these lost souls to suffer!"

The teacher saw a demon's fear crystalize as he came nearer and nearer the entrance to the bottomless pit. Everyone seemed frightened, except Satan and Death. The latter was standing at the entrance (but out of reach of Amadden) to see what would happen.

Both Death and the gatekeeper had raced on to greet Satan. Death rushed with the gatekeeper because he had the notion that Mephistopheles wanted to talk to Satan without him being there. I must be there to explain what occurred on the path of perdition, Death thought, and not let Mephistopheles tell it his way.

Even the gatekeeper showed a sense of fear, uncertainty, as he looked on the unfolding scene. What is the Messiah going to do? Mephistopheles thought. "Is he going into that place?" His thoughts ran through his mind, but he kept a straight face. "After all, the boss and Death seem to be enjoying this, so they must know something that evades me."

The Messiah read the gatekeeper's mind, and it brought him another distraction from the pain, as he mused over what was going on in their minds. For me to know and for you to find out, he said to himself.

The Messiah crept nearer to the entrance of Tartarus in purposeful strides under the weight on his shoulders. Surprisingly, Amadden was making no effort to bind him. to the demon looked at Christ in a manner that indicated his fear. Satan saw it and wondered.

The demons, oblivious to what was being played out before their eyes, became more brazen and assailed Christ with insults not worthy of repeating. Although they feared what he was up to, they seemed to be gaining confidence, knowing that Satan was there encouraging them with his presence.

It could be seen that they thought the Messiah would be there for all eternity! On the other hand, for Judas Iscariot, the walk was uneventful; no one interfered with him in his agony. It was as if someone had given instructions not to interfere with him. Thus, he complied with the Messiah's command to follow him.

I think that he is in pain, Iscariot suspected. "It sounds like he is, and to think that I caused this."

The nearer the Messiah came to Tartarus, the fumes that emanated from it became stronger. His nostrils were impacted with the spiritual and mental stench of it all. He said to himself, "Two more days and nights of this I must undergo. But, Satan, you will never see this pain. You will never know the cost that is being extracted even now. The price of man's redemption is very costly, but the benefits will outweigh the cost."

And Christ smiled in anticipation. Right then, he thought of Adam and Eve and knew how they felt even in paradise. They too had paid a price that no other humans had been asked to pay up to this point. As a form of distraction, Christ decided to reach out to those who were on the other side waiting for his coming.

Now that is the sweet aroma of anticipated victory, he thought, one that Satan will never relish throughout all eternity.

And with that thought in mind, Jesus turned and smiled at Satan and Death, who seemed intent on following him stride for stride to the edge of the precipice. Thus, he said to himself, somewhat in consolation, "You two will pay dearly. I promise you that."

Jeremiah, who is the commentator for those on the other side of the void, asked him a question. "Teacher, Master, who is that demon who is standing at the entrance so transfixed? And why are those around not going near him? Is there something that we ought to know of him?"

"There is nothing that you really have to worry about him," Jesus answered. "He is over here, and you are over there. Those who are over here cannot go over there, and vice versa. You are protected.

"Still, his name is Amadden, the guardian of the pit, Tartarus. He keeps the most dangerous of demons locked down there!"

The humans who lined the walkway on both sides of him spoke up, admonishing the demons who were tormenting Christ. But Christ himself was more involved with another unfolding celebration. And this one tickled his heart and brought a smile to his lips.

"It works! Adheres and John had done it. I can hear the rejoicing coming into my mind as they welcome Adheres.

"I only wished that Judas had asked forgiveness so that he did not have to be here. But he made his choice, and both of us must accept it. Now he is on his way to that part of Hades, Tartarus, which was designed for the most evil." At that moment, John reached out to him and asked about Judas following behind. The Messiah smiled as their minds linked. Christ said, "Judas is on his way to his ultimate payoff for selling me out! He is bound for Tartarus!"

"Give him a hand!" a voice shouted.

The scream brought the Messiah's mind racing back to the present situation, and he faced Satan. "I do not need any assistance! If I needed help, I would not have come here to get it!"

Satan had asked one of the demons to assist the Messiah to the entrance of Tartarus, but Christ would have none of it. Moreover, none of them wanted to be near Amadden if they could help it.

"It would mean that I'm incapable of doing this on my own as my father expected. I'm well able to perform my duties; thank you!"

This statement caught Satan's attention, and he visibly flinched. He knew then that things might not work out the way he had envisioned. Something invaded the devil's consciousness and bravado at that moment, something that would not let go, something that would not come into the light of understanding. Satan looked over at Death and the gatekeeper, who had come up and stood there watching the proceedings and saw, for the first time, a hint of worry.

"What's this?" Satan said frightfully. "Even Death is showing signs of worry, as if he too is fighting to bring something into clarity.

"I do not get it!" continued Satan. "Death, is there something that we have missed?"

Death, on the verge of answering, felt the invisible force coming to bear on his mind, numbing his every power of thought. And so he glanced at the devil and said, "No. Not to my knowledge!"

Nothing came clear to Death and Satan, and for once, they were not only stumped but also getting anxious and angry.

What is it that is playing tag with my mind? the devil thought. Again he looked at Death, only to see the same look of consternation on Death's face.

Meanwhile, Christ kept walking with purpose toward Amadden and Tartarus, that wide opening that descended into the very bowel of Hades. Nothing of the interaction among Satan, Death, and the Messiah missed Amadden. He was privy to what was going among the three: Satan, Death, and the Messiah.

"I do not know what is happening, but I do know that the Messiah's being here spells trouble," concluded Amadden. "I can feel it permeating every part of me. And it is troubling these two also. He is in control, and there is nothing that they or I can do.

"I have never seen Satan and Death in such a pitiful position before. Look at Satan, he is actually trembling. Not that I'm any different but these two . . . To think that they have been afraid of me, not wanting to get close to me. Hmm . . ." Amadden mused.

Judas Iscariot came behind and was in more pain with each step that he took following Christ. "I followed him when we were both alive. At first, I did believe in him; I was conscientious. So where did I go wrong? What caused me to be here now following him at the wrong time?"

As Judas was asking himself the question, he involuntarily glanced at Satan, who looked back at him with a smile. Iscariot knew then beyond any doubt who was responsible for his demise. It was as if a film of darkness had been lifted from his eyes, and subsequently, his anger rose. The look that he gave the devil said it all. Judas Iscariot was beyond anger; he was livid and began to curse.

Satan was visibly displaying anger where there should have been joy. This was not lost on his minions who stood around mocking, pushing, and hitting Christ as he passed by. Had they looked more closely at Christ, they would have seen the whimsical smile that played along the corners of his lips.

"They do not even know that my presence is affecting their minds in a way that they have never before experienced," Jesus spoke while musing. "This is the beginning of the end, Satan, and you feel it creeping in but not know it, cannot explain it, Can you?" Then as he scanned their minds, he read the questions and subsequent answer that Judas experienced. This caused him to turn around and looked at the two in question, Judas and the devil.

"Judas, meet your father. However, you will have time to converse with him later, but not now. You go to a place where you will spend the rest of eternity."

Then Christ thought to himself, I wonder if the devil realized what I just implied. "Hmm . . . Oh yes, Satan, where this, your child, is going is where you too will go in due time!"

Judas was transformed into another person, different from the one that had followed Christ in life and recently in death. Hell was doing something to him that he was yet unaware of. He had fulfilled his role as the son of perdition, but now Hades is taking over. Judas began to fit in, not anymore trying to induce Christ to forgive and reprieve him.

The mouth of Tartarus, and Amadden was getting ever so close. Although they wondered why Christ would go toward it, they also did not try to stop him, knowing what awaited him. As the lip of Tartarus loomed closer, it became deathly quiet. None of the demons who had been harassing Jesus seemed to want to venture any closer to Amadden and Tartarus. In the past, many demons had made that mistake and paid dearly for it. On such occasions, Amadden usually became like an eagle ripping a small chicken apart. Thus, the demons stopped short of its entrance. They were afraid of venturing any closer to what they knew inhabited it.

They are ingrained with the premonition of what is to happen at the end when they are judged, Jesus thought. "For that reason, they are staying as far as possible away from it and its keeper!"

The moment of truth is at hand, Jesus said to himself, and he looked at Judas one more time. "This is it, Judas. This is what you had worked so hard to accomplish for your father. Are you not pleased?"

With that stinging remark, the teacher turned toward the mouth of the worst part of Hades and came face to face with Amadden. Those who were closest to Jesus heard his statement and thought that he was talking of his pending entrance. But that had nothing to do with it. Instead, the Messiah was reminding Judas of what Satan had done to him. Christ was likewise thinking of judging and sentencing Death and Satan in the near future.

Amadden did not try to stop Christ but reached for Judas. "Come to me; I have been waiting for you."

And Judas screamed. He dodged the outstretched hands of the demon by flitting to the other side of the Messiah. Messiah then mind linked with Amadden and spoke to him. "This I want to do: I want to bind him down there myself for what he has done, so let him follow me. He is doing something that he didn't do in life: to follow me. Now he must follow me to his last abode."

With that, Amadden stepped back and allowed them passage untouched. Judas, as he neared the entrance, felt the grip of a fear which exceeded any that he had so far encountered. And he began to tremble violently and cry again, thinking how much he had lost and could not regain. Then without any warning, he started cursing again, but more extensively this time. Jesus said to himself, Now, that is the real Judas standing up to be recognized. "He sounds so much like those whom he is going to join soon!"

Had Judas heard that last statement, he would have realized how dismal his situation was and, more important, how evil he had become. He was to be chained alongside the most infamous of all demons and humans the earth had ever experienced.

Abruptly, Christ came to a standstill, and all the demons thought that he had finally become scared of entering—like they were. However, that was not the reason for his abrupt standstill. He needed to confide in John and Abraham before entering Tartarus for a night and day.

Meanwhile, because Christ had stopped so suddenly, Amadden was able to get his hands on Judas, who screamed as if he were in more pain than he was already suffering.

"It is not a physical pain, Judas," Jesus said. "It is fear, hatred, and hopelessness attacking you as he touches you."

"Messiah, make him go away!"

"You dug the hole, Judas. Now step into it!"

Then Jesus looked at Amadden, who released his hold on Judas. Then Jesus turned his attention to those on the other side of the void.

They must know that I will return and that this is just a stop on the way back to the father, Jesus mused. "I must assure them that I will be there in paradise to take them home with me. They need this assurance. I can feel their minds trying to grasp my absence for a day out of their sight, and their minds are closed to this place of all places. All humanity, including those in paradise, will be in a state of flux until I reappear. But for those in paradise, it means leaving that place in Hades for a heavenly trip that is one-way. I cannot leave without giving them this assurance."

With that in mind, Christ reached out to John the Baptist to console him and, through him, the others, including Abraham and Adam. "Hello, John! Hello, Abraham! Adam! How are you?"

"Teacher? Messiah!"

Simultaneously, they responded to his voice in their heads. And this got the attention of all who was there. They all spoke in unison. They were talking to the Messiah!

Adam was the first to ask a question, which provoked the interest of all the people who were waiting for his appearance. "Where is he?" "Is he all right?" "Is there anything that we . . . I can do?"

Christ heard every question that he asked, and responded directly. "No, Adam, there is nothing that any of you can do. Simply wait until I return to give each of you an opportunity to accept me as the only begotten son of the father. Right now, I must go and take care of the rest of this promise. So, until I return in a day, do nothing but enjoy your pending release.

"Adam, be kind to yourself. This will all be over, and you will be vindicated—both you and Eve—for the trick that Satan played on you. I must enter this pit now to confront those who thought to make your descendants their puppets.

"Abraham, take Adam and give him a hug. He has been through more than others. And Adam, please embrace Eve also. Do not blame her for this either. You must let her off the hook. She too has been through a lot."

Abraham closed his loving arms around Adam just as he hugged his wife Eve. All will be well, folks," Abraham said.

Then the celebration in paradise really began.

"The Messiah will be here soon!" they all chanted.

Christ turned to the entrance of Tartarus and took his first step into the void with Amadden and Judas following closely. Amadden was not acting like in control of this sector of hell but as one who took orders from the Messiah. The smell of evil closed in around them, and the Messiah felt as if he was choking.

The evil that emanated from Tartarus was vile and had a rancid smell. It was the breath of death. The thousands of demons exhaled and held for what seemed to be eternity what was left in their lungs.

Christ descended slowly with his burden rocking precariously on his back and shoulders. Judas followed, not wanting to go but unable to avoid taking the steps. Amadden followed them, which was not customary for him. All eyes were on the Messiah—ignoring Judas—as the Lord's second step took him past the entrance, and then he began the descent to the bottom. Then with a rousing crescendo the demons began to laugh.

"Satan has really won!" "Satan has defeated the Messiah." "He should have taken his offer, and he would not have to enter Tartarus."

Judas, following the Lord, looked back one more time and screamed most loudly. Then all eyes focused on him. Death turned to Satan and saw the anger and frustration on Lucifer's face as he looked at Judas.

"I cannot stop this. I cannot stop this! Why?"

"Stop what? The teacher?" asked Death.

"No, fool. I cannot stop him from taking the son of perdition into the depths with him."

The group, standing around the entrance and laughing, did not know that Christ wanted to go there of his own accord. They gave him no chance of survival because of the demons that shared the recesses of the pit. They held no hope that he would return and that they would eventually be staying in Tartarus forever. And so after Christ had descended with his burden, things went back to normal for the demons and the human residents. Meanwhile, Judas found himself being pulled as if by a magnet, one that would not allow him to lag behind but pulling him down deeper and deeper into the hole of Tartarus.

Still, outside the gates of Tartarus, Darkness waited patiently. He knew that he had been drawn there but did not know the reason, so he waited.

Etchers's Dilemma

"The worms do not die. They just crawl around, some seeking . . . to get into my skin. What kind of . . . worm . . . does . . . not . . . die in this . . . intense heat . . . and fire?"

And that was the only time Etchers had to question because the next instant he felt the gnawing pain from one of the worms that began gnawing inside his small intestines. One of the worms had already furrowed into his body, trying to eat and at the same time make a home for itself. His scream was heard throughout perdition and prompted the demons to laugh. The gatekeeper peered down to where Etchers was and chuckled. "You should have paid more attention to whatever the Messiah said to your friend Adheres, and most likely, you would not be here now."

Etchers had fared a little better than Judas, who had been dragged into the pit. As a matter of fact, he was now chained right beside some of those that he knew had conducted the same kind of business as he and Adheres. And as it was with them, he too began suffering the same fate.

"If I had only done what Adheres had done. I too would be where he is now! I'm sure that he is better off than I."

Just then, he looked up from his torment and saw Adheres on the other side of the void hugging and dancing with others who seemed to be enjoying themselves immensely.

The others, noticing the direction in which he was looking, indicated that this was a part of their punishment—to be able to see those on the other side enjoying themselves.

"But why do you look at that man over there?" Etchers was asked. "Do you know him?"

"Of course, I do! That is Adheres, my partner in crime!"

"What?"

The response from those around him was simultaneous. "Then why is he there, and you here?"

Etchers bowed his head in shame and agony. "I did not listen to what the Messiah told him!"

"And what was it that he said to him that caused him to be there now, and you here?"

"Oh, I mocked the Messiah along with the people who were crucifying us, but he admonished Adheres and me to join them. At which point Adheres said to the Messiah, 'Lord, remember me when you come into your kingdom.' And Jesus said to him, 'Assuredly, I say to you, today you will be with me in paradise!'"

"Oh? Then something is wrong because this Jesus just passed us on his way to the pit, followed by Amadden. No one comes back from that pit—no one! Still, why is your friend over there and both you and him—this Jesus—are over here? What gives? Does he think that he will leave here and further escape the pit? That is not possible! Something is wrong with that picture!"

"Why do you say something is wrong?" Etchers asked the demons.

"Oh that is simple. Your friend is over there, which is paradise. Unless there is something more which you are not telling or you have missed."

"I did not miss anything except my senses. I talked to Adheres all the way here, and gradually, it was as if our paths separated. He was on my right side and kept drifting away from me! Death and Confusion tried to grab him—to no avail. He just kept drifting away. I now know that the right side leads to paradise, and the left side to this place."

Silence then enveloped the group for a short time, later broken by an exclamation from one of those sitting there.

"It must be true! It must be true! He must be able to leave this place and go over there. Think about it. How calm was he when went by us? Looking so confident! It surprised me, but I did not pay much attention to it. He must be the Messiah and have the ability to leave here when he is ready!"

"Hmm . . . that makes sense!" another demon commented. "We are fortunate to be here where it leads directly to the gate, so when he comes back from the pit, we will be directly across from him. We can then petition him to take us with him!"

The statement caused Etchers to feel much better. Then he remembered the conversation that occurred between himself and the Messiah. He opened his mouth to say that it would not happen but decided to abstain. I am not going to say anything, the former thief thought. "They may get angry and decide to beat me. I will not give them any reason to want to turn on me."

The group became jubilant in expectation of the Messiah's return, but they still had to deal with the burrowing worms, the heat, the fire, and the demons. The demons saw them in conversation but paid them no attention at the time. However, now they were more than curious because they seemed to be less agitated.

"Something is wrong over there!" one demon commented.

However, it was downplayed as another demon commented in jest that the group might think that they had an opportunity to escape this place. "Leave them alone to their fantasy. It is a temporary relief for them!"

The rest of the demons broke out laughing hilariously. Meanwhile, Etchers continued to look in the direction of Abraham's bosom. His thoughts took on a different problem as he perceived the festive atmosphere over there. "How is it that . . . I . . . can . . . see . . . that far off? Adheres! Adheres! Oh, he cannot hear me. I'm done for! This mind link does not work!"

Adheres, hearing as if from afar the voice shouting his name, looked around and saw Etchers way off in the distance among the fires of Hades. His friend was writhing in pain. "Etchers, what can I do for you?"

"Oh, it does work."

"You know that I cannot cross over to you!"

"I know that," Etchers replied. "But why didn't you get my attention more on that cross when you spoke to the Messiah? Why didn't you? Now, here I'm suffering, and there you are, enjoying! It is not fair!" As he paused in pain, a worm bit into another of his smaller intestines.

Adheres responded to the question. "You had your chance! It was the same chance that I received. But to the end, you listened to those who could not help you. You didn't even consider that anything would have been better at that moment in your sorry life. I tried to warn you that we were guilty and he was not, but you wouldn't pay any attention to me or him. I'm sorry, Etchers, but you made your choice even when you had nothing to lose except ask him to remember you also, just in case what has been said about him was correct. I did. I believed, and because I did, here I end, and there you are. What is more, it is all fixed and cannot be changed. Good-bye, Etchers!"

One of those who were chained with Etchers looked over and said to him, "You had an opportunity to escape this evil place while you were hanging on the cross, but you did not accept it. Tell me that I did not hear your former friend right. Tell me that you chose to be here of your own accord."

With that said, Etchers began howling as more worms entered his body and chewed at his insides. "Oh, the pain," he wailed. "When will it stop?"

"At the end of eternity," one of the onlooking demons responded. "It will stop at the end of eternity."

This made Etchers's situation even more painful, and he cried out in agony, not only because of the pain that the worms and the fire had caused but because of the length of time he had to endure it all. Then he remembered everything that had occurred which led him to this moment of time in eternity. "I can see my life and the things that I have done, but I wonder . . . Adheres? How will you explain your sins that we committed together?"

"Do not worry about me Etchers," Adheres answered. "I was told by the Messiah that I will have no more sins to contend with because he has taken them with him. Do you remember the load that he carried as he walked down the road of perdition? My sins were in that baggage, under which he strained. And yours would have been also, if you had accepted the gift that he extended to both of us. Yes, he took my sins with him to Tartarus. Though there were many which you and I committed together, he chose to take them with him and free me from their bondage. I'm free, Etchers. I'm free!"

The conversation was not going the way that Etchers wanted it because all that he got out of the conversation with Adheres was more pain and hopelessness. "Eternity . . . eternity . . . such . . . a . . . long . . . time!"

A demon near Etchers began mocking him but suddenly stopped. "Something about that statement told me that we demons may have more than we think waiting for us. I must ask the devil, Satan, about this because suddenly I feel that we are going to be there and feeling the same kind of pain as these humans." This brought a degree of sobering to the demon's demeanor, to which he turned away from Etchers and the other humans and proceeded to pace, as if irritated.

"What has gotten into him?" The question came from Etchers, without him realizing that he had asked it. The other demons who stood around seemed to pick up for the first time the significant change in the demon's behavior, and they were astonished.

"What is it? What is wrong with you?" For a split second, the demons completely forgot the humans, concentrating solely on their fellow and crowding around him.

"Do you realize that if this Messiah is ever allowed to leave here, we would be in the same situation as these humans?" the demon asked.

A cloud seemed to descend on the group of demons in that moment of time. However, it was momentary as this reverie was broken up by the presence of Mephistopheles striding toward them.

"What is this? What is the communion about?" the gatekeeper asked the group. "Why are you congregating like this, without concern for your charges? Have you forgotten what is expected of you? I know what you are thinking because as you are, so are many others like you. And I will not allow that to happen. Not while I guard that gate! Moreover, if Satan realizes that you are conferring about this, he will rip you apart!"

"If we are right, that may not be a bad way to go!" one demon remarked. "Consider, spending all eternity in the same dilemma as these humans."

The statement had a disastrous effect on the gatekeeper, and in order not to show its effect, he turned and started lashing out at them. The demons in turn started lashing out at the humans who were stationary in their positions. Etchers became the focus of many of them as they blamed him for this new trend of thought, causing Christ who was on his way down to the bottom of Tartarus, to smile.

Etchers's cries to the onslaught that he took could be heard throughout Hades. His attackers bore him no mercy. The more they beat him, the more they thought of what was now inextricably lodged in their minds. "All eternity . . . all eternity . . . all eternity!" This was their speech as they continued to pound on him. "I will be here for all eternity . . . All eternity? We will have to spend all eternity in this same situation as you humans, you . . . unwitting idiots?"

Adheres, on the other side with the ever watchful Jeremiah, saw the onslaught on Etchers but found that the feeling he had for this man had waned to almost nothing.

"Your former associate just took a licking, Adheres!" Jeremiah said. "That he did, didn't he?"

Etchers was beaten into a senseless stupor yet with knowledge of what was happening to him. He was completely aware and sensitive to every blow that fell on him from powerful hands but could do nothing about it. Adheres, after conversing with Jeremiah about it, said, "There but for the grace of God I go. To think that at the last moment, even while Christ was suffering, he gave me this gift of salvation. Otherwise, I could have been right there beside Etchers receiving the same punishment!"

For a brief moment in time, Adheres felt the pain of empathy, but only for a brief moment as Jeremiah placed his arms around his shoulders and said, "I too would have been, if it was not for that same grace from the father—God!"

His response brought Adheres comfort, and they looked at each other and laughed. Abraham, who looked at both, heard what they said, and having also witnessed the onslaught on Etchers, joined them and said, "Gentlemen, this is what salvation is all about! When I sinned—by allowing myself to lust after Sarah's hand maiden—I too caused a whole flood of misdeeds to come on Israel. But for the grace of God, I am here."

"We are all indeed blessed to have God on our side, aren't we?" said Jeremiah.

And Darkness waited, ever patiently.

Christ had disappeared for quite some time. Meanwhile, there was a group of hardier demons hanging around Tartarus's entrance, waiting, hoping that they would hear something. Satan had returned to his lair with a mixture of triumph and pensiveness in his mind.

"I do not understand," Satan said. "But this I do know—no one goes down to that pit and come back. NO ONE!"

The feeling that something was amiss did not leave Lucifer. But he was not to be outdone in this celebration, and so he joined his entourage in more celebration. The hardy demons hung around the entrance per chance they could have something that they could take back to Satan as a proverbial feather in their cap. But there was nothing. Besides, Amadden had followed the Messiah into Tartarus, so they were somewhat confident, standing so close to Tartarus's entrance.

"He is never coming back from that place. Amadden will see to that!" stated one of them.

"You think so? I looked at him as he walked into that entrance, and I must tell you, he seemed rather confident, assured that he will not be there for long!" said another.

And so the conversation went back and forth among them as they lounged about the entrance.

Judas screamed, and it was heard by the onlookers at the entrance to Tartarus. This caused them to jump, half expecting to see Amadden's face appear above the pit's entrance. But that was not to be. Amadden had simply grabbed Judas, and the latter in response wailed with pain and in convulsion. Amadden's touch achieved that kind of reaction from others, no matter who it was. The demon had thought of also touching the Messiah but couldn't. There seems to be some kind of protective force around him, I wonder, Amadden thought.

"Amadden, if you touch me, I will feel the same pain as does Judas," came the Messiah's words in mind link.

Yet Amadden could not bring himself to touch him. Maybe if I am good to him, he will be merciful to me when the time comes, mused the demon.

There was no expectant crying out from Christ. There was the usual howling from the demons that everyone knew were chained in Tartarus. The only other howls that were distinctly identifiable, other than the usual inhabitants, were that of Judas cursing extensively.

"What gives? How long before he reaches the bottom?" one demon asked.

One demon answered and said, "Is that why you are hanging around here? Don't you know that this is a bottomless pit?"

"Yes, I know that it is, but I figure that with all that weight that he seemed to be carrying, he may have dropped like a piece of lead to the farthest reaches by now?"

The Messiah took his time walking down the steep precipice, not wanting to reach the end of the journey before its allotted time. It was a part of the price that he agreed to pay, and he was making sure that all of it was paid for the purchase of mankind as preordained.

"Ah! Judas, your true self is emerging so brilliantly!" Jesus said.

"Messiah, you did know that I would betray you when you chose me?"

"Yes, I did! I knew that you would betray me, and you would have done it sooner, if the Holy Spirit did not deny you the opportunity before you did! Yes, Judas, I knew all along, and so did the father—that is why he chose you to be my disciple."

Iscariot now had a voice that was changed, no more whining, but more gruff, and the curses that came from his mouth said a lot about what was in his heart. The time period to get to the ultimate part of Tartarus was not measured as humans measured time, but in terms of the cost of sins.

The more sinful—the more egregious the sin—the longer it took to reach the lowest depths. Christ carried more sin than any one person did, because he had past, present, and future sins all stacked on his back. Subsequently, the price that was being exacted was more than anyone could imagine in terms of pain. Unfortunately for Judas, his time was also extended because he had to walk behind the Messiah to the journey's end.

"It was an exorbitant sum, but I, the Messiah, was willing to pay every denary of it. It is worth it! I must suffer so that man will not, if they choose, suffer, by confessing me as the only begotten son of the father," Jesus said to himself as he made his way down to the final resting place of man's sins.

"You are God's only begotten son. You can do anything you want!" Judas said. It irritated the Messiah to hear that comment from him.

"You will say no more from this moment on, demon! You will follow me until I order you to stop—that is all that you will do! Do you understand?"

Judas Iscariot did not answer. He couldn't because his mouth was closed, and not by his own doing.

Your master trained you so well that you would take it on yourself to try and tempt me, even here!" Then Messiah went back to his musing.

Amadden, following closely, thought of Judas, "I 'm going to have fun with this one when the Messiah leaves . . . Hmm, what caused me to think that? How is he going to leave this place? No one had ever left here. Oh, on occasion Satan would come down here, I think, as a form of a reminder for something—I don't know what. But he never stayed here for any length of time, and I know that he feels pain when he does. So why do I think that he—the Messiah—will leave? This is strange . . . this . . . is . . . strange!"

The Messiah, while leading the way, smiled. "These occupants are the ones who perpetuated the worst crime, the worst sins, of having illicit relationships with women and caused such disharmony among men over and above what Satan had already done."

And so from the moment that the Messiah started down the incline of Tartarus, pain radiated throughout Tartarus's inhabitants in their chained positions. This too was part of their punishment, as well as that of Iscariot's. They felt every step that Christ took because they were intricately attached to the ground of Tartarus in a symbiotic relationship.

And even more than Satan and Death, the inhabitants knew why they were feeling this inexorable pain as sin drew closer to them. They had corrupted so many of the people that God could not allow them to continue. Moreover, they had acted according to Satan's master plan to produce a type of human that would acknowledge only him and his ideals.

These men and women were so different from the normal masses; they were extraordinary people in that they stood taller than all others. They were giants!

These demons cannot leave until the last days when they would be let out for a time. God does not want them to contaminate the earth any more than they already did. The sin for which they were judged holds them bound to and inseparable from Tartarus. Consequently, although the burden (mankind's sin) was heavy, it was also a punishment to them as the weight on Christ caused his feet to sink into the side of Tartarus on his downward trek.

Soon the voices of the pit-bound demons could be heard—groans and moans. The suffering of the chained demons became clearer as Christ kept walking down. The groans and moans became more audible, and their cursing could be heard even though he was some distance from them.

"You have brought this on yourselves, so now you must bear the consequences," Jesus said. "You could have stayed in heaven if you did not lust after the things that Satan painted for you. You would not have been here now."

On the teacher's way down, he had listened to the conversation that occurred between Etchers and Adheres. It was a conversation that caused him some distraction from the ever intense pain that he was undergoing. Still, it served as a constant reminder of the reason he was here at this particular place. Both had made their choices and now are being given their eternal reward.

As the teacher traveled down to Tartarus, he kept thinking of Judas, his companion for the moment. Thus, he mused, "And you, Judas, will also join these inhabitants in Tartarus because of your

betrayal of the only begotten son of the father—God. You have
been pronounced as the son of perdition, and for that reason, your
betrayal carries the penalty of eternal death, of the highest degree
of punishment. That is why I tried so hard to save you in those
last moment of your natural life. I had promise; my father had
promised that I would come and give my life as the sin sacrifice so
that whoever believed would be saved. I came to die for you, Judas,
and all who believe! But instead of believing that, you denied me
that right, the right to die for you."

Judas groaned even more!

"It should be about midnight," Satan thought. "He should be at
the deepest reaches of Tartarus by now. "I wonder how he feels now,
knowing that he will have to spend all eternity with those who are
below. I did not know that he would be really here—but he is—and
that opens the doors for me to now have my way."

The fire glowed with an eerie and surreal wickedness that could be
felt more intensely rather than seen. This fire, its intensity, transcends
any other fire that mankind had ever beheld. And as Satan sat in
contemplation over the fate of Christ, he thought of only two other
places where this kind of fire had been lit: Sodom and Gomorrah.
Sodom and Gomorrah, now there was a particularly savory victory,
Satan thought. "In one fell swoop, I made a coup that was so
astonishing that this so-called Lord had to come down and personally
deal with it. Now all its occupants, except Lot, are here. Now two more
coups on this day alone—Judas and Jesus the Christ!"

Satan should have known then who made those fires and who
subsequently made the fire that was around him. It should have
been a warning to him, but it was not.

"It was a pleasure for me to convert Judas, one of his disciples,
into his traitor. Iscariot was so easily toppled off his high horse of
pride and materialism. Did he not know that this is the first of many
sins that I introduced to mankind? He never listened when Christ
spoke. He was always using the poor as a reason for something
while pertinent information kept passing him by. Now he knows
what he had done. And as I perused them, I knew that he was the
one. He was so materialistic!

"I intend to make this place more for this Messiah than for any other person whom I have here."

Nevertheless, the demons who were there when the Messiah stepped into the pit thought for a moment that Christ was in control, and not he, Satan.

"I offered him so much if he would bow down and accept me as his master, but no—I was not good enough for him. He kept quoting me scriptures. Well, Mr. Big Shot, wait, until I start quoting for you some of those same scriptures and see what happens."

Christ, almost to the end of his journey into Tartarus, smiled at his words and started anticipating the end results. That smile was like a promise of what he would do to this devil when he returned to Hades proper.

Just then he, Satan, heard the screams. They were not the ordinary screams that he was used to hearing—they were different. Naturally, Satan attributed them to Christ, but he was wrong again. The screams came from the chained demons as they realized who was purposely coming down the side of Tartarus—Christ. And so their pain intensified a thousandfold.

Christ, the only begotten son of the father, had entered Tartarus, the most punishable area of perdition. Those who were housed in its cavernous sides were the beneficiaries of his entrance.

However, Satan and Death did not know what was transpiring. All they thought was that it was Christ screaming in the agony of defeat.

Pain, unadulterated pain, seeped into every tissue of the demons' bodies and caused them to howl and wail beyond anything that they could ever have experienced.

"Please, go back!" they cried. "We know that we are being punished, but we did not expect you here this soon. Leave us alone. We are suffering enough!"

The Messiah had no pity for them because he too was suffering from the intensity of pain brought on by the shame and weight of mankind's sins. Yes, he would be glad to leave when it was over.

The Messiah reached the end of his journey down the side of Tartarus and carefully down placed the conglomeration of sins. It was the dawn of the first day, but for Christ, it was like the beginning of eternity. He held strongly to his commitment to the father and, subsequently, to humanity.

Every sin had to be unloaded and placed carefully so that they can fall into the bottomless pit, where they will be most effective in causing pain as they float in the seamless void around these culprits. It was punishment for the present residents of Tartarus, and also a gift for Satan and his fellow demons.

As had been foretold, a number of other humans would join Iscariot here, along with those who were already there. Of course, those who were already there were also feeling the agony of unremitted sins. This place was prepared for the most evil men and women of the past, present, and future; indeed, those who disdained God, Christ, and the Holy Spirit, and catered to the anti-Christ and Satan.

It will be one of the happiest days of my life to see Satan, Death, the anti-Christ all in one place being punished for all eternity, Jesus thought. "It will be the apex of my joy, in addition to spending the rest of my life with those who have confessed me."

Christ, resting from his purposeful and long walk into Hades and down to its uttermost part, was lost to the sounds around him, until one demon asked him if he was really the Messiah.

"Oh, don't you know?" Jesus answered. "After all that you did with my father's people while confronting me, you still do not know me? I know all of you, and yet you do not know me! I'm your judgment and the redeemer of mankind whom you tried to turn into the evil that you and your master are. Yes, you are correct in this assumption—I am the Messiah and soon to be king of kings."

"Why are you here already?" the demon asked. "Has the world come to an end? Have you come to give us freedom?"

"No, the world has not yet come to an end, and I did not come here to set you free," Jesus replied. "I came to bring here all the sins of mankind, those who have accepted me as the Christ their savior, the only begotten son of the father. These are their sins, of which I have relieved them so that they can spend eternity with me, my father, and his holy spirit."

"And who is he, that one behind you? We do not know him!"

"Oh, he has come to join you for all eternity! He is the son of perdition," Jesus said. "You betrayed him, and then you were betrayed, right?"

"We are all in the same boat," the demons answered. "Satan said that he would fight for us, but here we are now, betrayed like you!"

"Judas, come along," Christ said. "I have a place here for you. Here you will spend all eternity, so you might as well get acquainted!"

With that, the Messiah then fastened Judas to the shackles that lay by the side of the wall of Tartarus.

"Satan rarely comes down here. But this is something that you already know! It is too much pain, even for him. Oh, I'm not surprised, but he will be coming down soon to see how I'm doing. He thinks that he will enjoy it."

And so the dialogue between the demons and Christ continued as he unloaded every sin into Tartarus and watched them float around the demons. With each sin placed in Tartarus, the pain and anguish of the demons increased, causing them to make even louder noises.

Etchers, working at easing his pain beside the others, looked in the direction of Tartarus and asked, "What is it that you think is happening down there?"

"I tell you this," answered someone beside him, "That the demons are afraid to go down there—even Satan. Sometimes he would go to the entrance and look down as if steeling himself to go down, but he never really does."

Another lost soul chimed in and began to speak. But while he spoke, the pain that he felt was registered in every part of his body, and could be seen in his face. He said, "The demons that are caged down there are the worst that you can ever imagine. They are not the demons to meet. By the way, did I not see you come through the gate with all the others? Were you not in the company of the other one who followed the Messiah down to the pit?"

"Yes!"

"Who is he that he was taken to the pit? He is not a demon, is he?"

"Actually, he was one of the Messiah's disciples!"

"Are you saying that he is relegated to the pit because he was one of Messiah's disciples?"

"No! He was dragged there because he sold the Messiah for thirty pieces of silver!"

"Thirty pieces of silver? Thirty . . . pieces . . . of . . . silver? Is silver that expensive now that the life of a man, particularly the Messiah's, is only worth that much? I remember that during Solomon's days, silver was something of very little value. When I robbed someone who had silver, I felt deprived and threw it back at them!"

"That sum is not expensive," Etchers explained. "He probably just hated the Messiah and decided to get rid of him. I don't think that the money was important. He was simply misguided by the devil."

"That man is an idiot," the unfortunate human said.

"Oh, he himself recognized it. That is why he is here—he killed himself."

"And now he pays a price that is very exacting—Tartarus—a place that I would not wish on my worst enemy."

With that remark, the three of them became silent as they worried about the constant pain that they were experiencing.

Etchers was in too much pain to really care that Judas brought it all on himself. "So like me, he deserves what he is getting." He tried to block out the pain that Judas voice, emanating from Tartarus, registered on him—to no avail. So Etchers in turn screamed and grabbed at his stomach. One of the worms bit savagely into his small intestine, ripping it apart. Funny, he commented to no one in particular. "They bite, but I do not bleed. Or I do not think so. It feels as if every bit of moisture had been sucked out of my flesh and bones. And to think that I have to experience this for all eternity. "What a mess I have made of my life."

Meanwhile, Christ completed the task of carefully placing each individual sin in Tartarus and smiled through the pain as he went through the tedious job of doing it. He thought to himself, This is worth it. "No one who enters this pit will ever get a moment's rest from the agony and the pain that they will experience."

The demons, on the other hand, felt every weight of sin as each one was carefully laid. The meticulous manner of the Messiah's approach to his task brought an intricacy of pain that was unrivaled. For all eternity the demons would experience excruciating pain, the pain of the sins which they had caused.

This is not sadistic on my part, Jesus reasoned with himself. "But when I realize what those who come here have caused, I believe they deserve it."

It was the end of the dawn of the first of three days. Two more nights for the Messiah in perdition. For Judas, it was the beginning of eternity of excruciating pain. This caused him to think that maybe his pain exceeded that of others.

Dawn of the First Day in Hades

Satan became anxious. He wanted to know what was happening to the Messiah in the worst part of Hades. However, there was no one to satisfy his curiosity. He couldn't have chosen a better place for the Messiah, if he had herded Christ himself down there. He chose it for himself, Satan thought. "Still, I need to know. Maybe one of those who have been hanging around the pit's entrance can tell me something." And so Satan strode out of his lair intent on getting information which could make him feel more at ease.

The demons who were staying around the entrance had nothing to report. Besides, they were scared that Satan would take it out on them. The devil started yelling and lashing out at them.

"No news may be good news but not for me. My adversary is down in that pit, and there is no way to know other to send someone down or go there myself. Seems as if I must go down there to see how things are coming along. No one else will go, knowing the temper of Amadden. He will not allow them to return." And so Lucifer extricated himself from the party which had been going on all night in hell.

All the demons were having fun at the expense of those who were housed in this part of Hades. The thought that had been troubling the devil all night surfaced again, but still it was on the outer fringes of his mind.

"He has been here twelve hours but have not yet really said a word to me. That is insulting. After all, I'm in charge down here." I must know what is going on down there. I could order one or two of my minions to go and investigate, but it would be self-defeating to say the least."

The more Satan thought about it, the more he was convinced that this was a job for him only. "If I send any of them they will not be allowed to return. I must do this myself. After all, I was placed in charge of this place!" As the thought ran through his mind, he received an answer that further shocked him.

"You were never placed in charge; you were sent here as a prelude to what is to come."

The words caused him to jump involuntarily. He realized in that instant that somehow the Messiah had something to do with it.

Unknown to Satan, Christ continuously read his mind and knew exactly what he thought. Thus, the Messiah said to himself, No, Satan. "You are not in charge, and I do not owe you any respect—contrary to what your pride has led you to believe. You will see and hear from me soon enough." Christ was very much alive and was about his father's business. This was his assignment, and he endeavored to see it through to the very end.

Still, Satan started walking down the incline. "I may be able to have some fun in this."

It was morning, and the demons of Tartarus were in an uproar. The sins which were laid around their feet and up against their bodies had been very painful. Even Judas received a portion of the sin that the teacher had brought to Tartarus. His sins were now mixed with those that he had inherited from the Messiah and those which caused him much pain. The pain was so intense that he felt a reprieve when the teacher touched his mind. They were in intense agony. Watching it all, the Messiah envisioned how it would be for the anti-Christ, Satan, and Death when they were finally assigned to this pit.

"Judas, you have surely chosen the wrong side in this battle. Now you are about to experience more than ever the error of your ways, for all eternity. You saddened me by your choice, but my father's business, not mine, is my objective. In the father's admonition, there is no assistance for you." And that thought continued to sadden Jesus. "But I have some news for you. Your father Satan is on his way here. I am sure that both of you have a lot to say to each other."

Satan stretched out his arms when he came out of his lair, much like a lion coming out of his den to move his muscles for circulation.

The night has been one partying night, he thought. "But something just seems to stay on the edge of my consciousness, never coming into full view so that I can identify it. Ever since, he just walked past me and headed into that hole, something has gnawed at me. I cannot figure out what it is.

"Now there he is in Tartarus doing God knows what, while I have to put on a face of deceit for those who are around me. That is not fair; neither is it right. I must go down there and see what is going on!

"And I know that something is also worrying Death and the gatekeeper. I saw it in their eyes, although like me they too try to hide it from me. So I guess that it is up to me to investigate the situation and put my mind at ease."

Demons lined up along the way to Tartarus, as if expecting him to show up. Each was wondering if this was the day when he would enter into it to deride the Messiah.

Satan had ventured into Tartarus before, but never down to where the worst of the worst demons were chained. Most times he remained close to the entrance while listening to their screams. He knew that they blamed him for their demise but was unconcerned.

"Still, I must stay away from them. Otherwise, they would try to rip me apart." He thought that he had only wanted to experience some of what its inhabitants had been feeling in the past. "But this is different, something . . . as if . . . like a magnet seems to pull me . . . toward the entrance." Something had got hold of him mentally and wouldn't let go.

It was Christ exerting pressure on Lucifer's mental capabilities to force him into the pit for a confrontation. And so the devil stepped onto the side of Tartarus and began his slow descent.

One of these days I will go down to the bottom of that pit, he thought to himself. "Maybe today is the day. After all, my most prized catch is down there! What in Hades have driven him to go down there anyway? I did not command it, so why?" Again that pang of tension entered the fringes of his mind but never venturing into view. "Did I do something wrong? Did I forget something? Why is this invisible hold pulling me to this place? I . . . do . . . want . . . to go . . . now! I . . . change . . . mind!"

However, no matter how he tried to resist the force, it seemed that his feet had a power of their own, which was foreign to him. So the mental war which he tried to wage was to no avail. His feet kept moving down the aperture of Tartarus.

Lucifer's mind was not on business as usual this morning. "Actually, this is not business as usual. The son of the father is down here, and I can imagine what the father is thinking up there on his throne right about now. He is thinking, 'How did Satan win out against my son? How come I did not see this coming?' He is mad as hell, but no matter what, I'm savoring every moment of it. I should pay him a visit today. But something tells me that I do not want to be there now."

The hour moved on although time meant nothing down here to Satan and his demons.

"On the other hand, these misguided human miscreants are in the throes of it. They seem to be counting every second of every minute of every hour that comes and slips by. Their agony is my triumph, and I love it. But most of all, I have collected the prize of all eternity! Eternity . . . something about eternity . . . is . . . bothering . . . me." And he howled in frustration that he could not get a clear picture of what had so far avoided his consciousness, or the force that propelled him forward.

Satan was climbing down, walking, so deep in thought that he was unaware of how much time had passed in his descent. "What is this? I'm losing my marbles! This descent seems to be controlled but not by me! This one time in Tartarus seems to be planned . . . ordained . . . and I have . . . no say in . . . the matter! Somehow I feel that it is dangerous for me. Yet I must overcome this feeling, particularly now that the so-called Messiah is down there!"

With that thought in mind, Satan reacted negatively, seeking to strike out at the nearest demon, but he was all alone in this journey. "Why did they not stop me . . . get my attention before I started down this pit? Now here I am alone and going into that one place which I have done my best to avoid and not traverse unnecessarily. I had come down once, when Death brought Genghis Khan here. He had been one of my favorite human servants, doing a lot of damage among the humans. And so I had accompanied him a part of the way, notwithstanding Amadden's hold on him."

The demons, who stood around the entrance to Tartarus, did not have anything to report.

"What is going on? Has anything happened during the night that I should be aware of?" It was a rhetorical question because Satan knew that out of fear someone would have brought him any news. The gatekeeper was there but had nothing of value to report, except the increased hollering and howling which came from below.

All Hades have heard those screams, Satan thought. "I have heard them, so they are nothing of importance or new to me. I need to know if anything unusual occurred during the night!"

No, Lucifer, nothing occurred, was Satan's thought as he continued his descent, but that was not to be. "We thought that some of the screaming came from him, but there was no way to confirm it. I wish that he could scream right now so that I can know that he is being tormented by Amadden and this pit."

Satan had shrugged off the answer that the gatekeeper had given him, believing rather that Christ was being torn apart by the demons of Tartarus. That sounded more feasible to him. But it was not. And so Satan made an announcement that caught by surprise almost everyone within hearing of his intent.

"I must go down there to see how he is doing. Do you want to join me, Death?"

"No, Lord, I have to be going. So many people are dying; they need my attention."

"Meph, would you like to join me?"

"That would mean leaving the gates unguarded, Lucifer, and you would not want that, now would you?"

Satan knew that they were only excusing themselves because they did not want to be there.

"I will see you both when I come back. He was already feeling faint from being so near the entrance and began wondering why Amadden has not put in an appearance yet.

Christ sat down on one of the ledges of Tartarus. He was exhausted from exertion, but also more from the intense pain that he suffered.

Distraction is on its way, the Messiah consoled himself. "Satan is coming down to see me! Now that is a welcome distraction, seeing that I must stay here all day!"

Satan's descent was slow and painful. "It is good that those two did not come with me. I would not want them to see me suffering like this! It would give them thoughts of possibly overthrowing me! Oh! The pain! Still, I committed myself to coming down here, and I must!"

The devil tried to speed up his descent, but it was as if something or someone was directing his actions, causing him to move slowly. As he descended, the (foreign) pain he felt became even more intense.

"Oh! . . . I'm feeling . . . so awful . . . so . . . out . . . of control! . . . I . . . wonder . . . No! . . . If . . . I . . . am . . . feeling pain . . . then . . . he . . . has to be. Ouch! Whew! Must . . . move . . . faster . . . Get this . . . finished."

The pain brought even more indistinguishable thoughts which would not clarify themselves, just staying out of reach of clarity.

"What . . . is . . . this?" Straining, he tried even harder to bring them into form but could not. And with each succeeding try, the pain became even more intense; thus, he decided not to try anymore.

"Getting . . . closer . . . demons . . . must . . . know . . . that . . . I'm coming . . . cursing . . . calling . . . me . . . names! Must . . . be . . . careful . . . not . . . to . . . get close . . . to them . . . rip . . . me . . . apart."

Christ, listening to his mind, laughed aloud, causing the demons to halt their cursing and moaning, to see why he laughed.

"Why . . . are . . . you . . . laughing? Don't . . . you . . . feel . . . pain . . . also?"

"For me alone to know about my feeling pain. But I laughed because your master is on his way down to see how things are doing. And he is in dire straights because of the pain that he has to endure. I . . . would . . . like . . . to . . . hold . . . for . . . a . . . short . . . while!"

Several of the demons expressed that wish, and the Messiah smiled ruefully.

Satan came into sight, looking so unlike his debonair self. He was in deep pain, as could be seen by the look on his face.

"Ah! There you are, Satan, what kept you so long?" Jesus greeted.

"Messiah! You . . . are . . . free . . . of the . . . chains!"

"Lord," the demons called out, "please . . . hold . . . him . . . and . . . bring . . . him . . . over here! We . . . want to . . . have a . . . physical . . . conversation . . . with . . . him!" The demons were all straining at their chains, hoping to break them for this one instance, getting their hands on Satan. However, Satan was wrapped up in so much pain that he did not even know how dreadfully close he was to being torn apart by his associates. Lucifer groaned and mourned, but he was careful not to challenge his mind anymore. The pain he suffered when he tried was a constant reminder not to do so—at least not while he was down here.

"You are here for a while, Satan, so lean back and be comfortable and enjoy the temporary pain among your peers," Jesus suggested.

"You . . . do . . . not . . . look . . . any . . . worse . . . for . . . having . . . been down . . . here . . . all . . . night . . . How . . . come?"

"Is that what you came to see?" the Messiah asked. "You wanted to see how much damage and pain have been inflicted on me? Oh, you demon. Did I disappoint you? As you can see, I do know that what you thought of seeing has not occurred, so that should tell you something, shouldn't it, Satan?"

Satan did not respond. The pain and anguish that he bore at that moment was something that he wanted kept as a secret.

The hours passed, which were like a thousand eternities for both Satan and Christ. The only difference between the two was that Satan's demeanor showed how he felt. On the other hand, Christ sat calmly throughout the whole ordeal. He reconciled himself to the fact that this was required for mankind's salvation.

"It is almost evening, Satan. Shouldn't you be on your way back to your lair?" The words came through the mind link from Christ.

It was as if some invisible hand had released its hold on Satan because no sooner had the words been spoken by the Messiah than the devil sprang upward and began climbing back to Hades and his lair. Again the thoughts invaded the fringes of his mind, but he had learned not to entertain them—at least not while he was down here!

Judas stood up to leave with Satan but found that he could not move! "Aren't you taking me back with you?"

"I cannot," Satan responded. "Amadden would not allow you to leave once you are here."

With those words ringing in Judas's ears, Satan turned and began climbing. In midstride, he looked at the Messiah and commented, "You should have taken my offer back there in the desert. You would have been better off now!"

"Says who? You, Satan? You who must come back here and spend all eternity? You are telling me that I would have fared better doing what you say? You must be joking! I would rather be here with these now, than to have collaborated with you! Be gone before I concede to the wishes of your associates!"

Satan leaped up and started climbing immediately. He was in much pain but decided that he would not show it. Not to this Messiah or the others who would be waiting topside. His climb was uneventful, and it was night by the time he reached his lair.

This would be the longest night that Satan would ever spend. He was irritable all night, as question after question from Death and Meph assailed him. No one else dared ask him anything because they feared him. Yet they hung around, hoping for some morsel of information about this Messiah in Tartarus. Satan's bravado took control, as if by some signal.

"He is there and suffering, as anyone who goes down there does. I too suffered but am stronger than he, enough to overcome it. On the other hand, I do not think that he can. We will see! However, he has that choice, to come up and join me or stay there forever. It is his choice." Satan never thought that he would see the Messiah again, and this gave him courage, courage that would be short-lived.

Near midnight, Christ stood up, and Amadden, as if expecting his departure, rose also to bid him so long.

"I must be going now," Jesus said.

Judas also leaped to his feet, expecting to follow the Messiah back to the surface.

"No, Judas, you belong here. "This is where you will spend the rest of eternity. You have earned that right."

It was the first night, coming close to morning of the second day, and Christ was on his way up from the bottom of Tartarus. Every step he took upward was agonizing for its occupants. Judas Iscariot had changed completely because he too cursed with each step that the Messiah took. Their screams filled the morning as the Messiah's footsteps caused—although not deliberately placed—the inhabitants to feel pain.

"Why are you hurting us? Why are you deliberately causing us pain?"

What the demons had not realized was that his foot steps were now under the purity of a sinless man, who was inherently opposed to evil. Christ still felt the pain and suffering that he had to undergo as part of the cost of redemption. However, being free of sin was an inverse relationship for Hades and, more so, for Tartarus. Thus, the interaction between this sinless man and the sin-filled Tartarus caused a reaction which was contrary in the outcome and in action. As Christ climbed upward, he heard a familiar scream and knew that Judas was being tormented by Amadden.

Judas, you will be experiencing this for all eternity, the Messiah thought.

The Messiah's climb up from Tartarus was a series of painful steps for himself and the demons of Tartarus. The father hadn't forgotten the demons' crimes, starting with their rebellion in heaven and the fact that they had decided to make the daughters of mankind their concubines.

"It's payback time."

All these occurred because Satan wanted to be in charge. He was not satisfied with the vaunted position that the father gave him—he wanted more! "Now, he has more, more than he could ever imagine, and the cost is exorbitant."

Now, he is beginning to pay the cost, said the Messiah to himself as he emerged from Tartarus to meet Lucifer.

Satan, although he had emerged from Tartarus and felt relieved, couldn't shake the fact that the Messiah was in Tartarus unharmed and seemingly undaunted by the experience. He, Satan, had been there and bore excruciating pain which was unfamiliar to him, except for that one occasion when the father threw him out of heaven.

"That was a painful experience! I still smart from that encounter."

Now as he sat in his lair, he had realized that he was uncomfortable about all that has so far transpired. "I didn't even have a decent conversation with him all the time I was there. He did all the talking, and I simply listened! Ah! That was not my intent!"

As the morning drew near, Lucifer felt the urge to be someplace else. Where? He did not know, but he knew that it was someplace not his lair. And so he found himself walking aimlessly at first, and then with what was seemingly a destination in mind.

The pit, I must go there, Lucifer finally said. "I feel like I am being drawn to that place. Is this the working of Amadden? I think that I will have to have a conversation with him this time, one that will let him know who is really in charge here."

Still, the devil found himself being drawn to the pit's entrance, not being able to resist the urge. Consequently, he, Death, the gatekeeper, and many of the demon residents of hell were standing there when the Messiah emerged. A hiss went out of their mouths involuntarily, not knowing that they did.

"How did he get out? Where is Amadden? I am the only one who goes down there and return, so what gives here?"

The questions kept coming to his mind, and he could formulate no answers which could give validation to this apparition which he and his cohorts were witnessing.

"It cannot be!"

The news of Christ's reentry into Hades from the pit spread like wildfire, causing the hopes which some had cherished to return to the surface of their mind. Even Etchers, who should have known better, felt that maybe there was some hope. His fellow residents thought likewise.

When Christ came out of Tartarus, Jeremiah, across the way in paradise, announced it to those who were too far back to see for themselves the proceedings. The Messiah stopped and faced the crowd gathered around the entrance to Tartarus. And there was the devil looking brave, as if he was in charge.

"Now listen all of you," said Jeremiah. "The Messiah is tuned in to you so that you can hear with your minds what he is saying to the devil. This is the moment of truth for Lucifer!"

Satan stood a little way off from the entrance to Tartarus, having been physically shaken by his recent visit to the pit. It was an experience that he did not relish nor wanted to undergo again. He had not expected Christ to emerge from Tartarus, although he gave the demons the impression that he had given Christ a choice. Thus, Satan jumped involuntarily at the sight of Christ's head protruding from Tartarus.

No human had ever come up from that pit, and what Lucifer was now seeing did not sit well with him. To conceal his disappointment and what seemed to be some semblance of fear on his part, the devil forced himself to cover it up by going on the offensive in his speech.

"Ah, there you are! I . . . we were wondering when you would grace our company with your presence."

There was no word coming from the Messiah's lips. Instead, Christ chose to use his mind to connect with Satan and, in so doing, shut out all others but him. The only other people to hear what was about to transpire were the residents of Abraham's bosom.

Satan felt the power of the Messiah's mind touch him, and he winced unwittingly. Still, his reaction and how he felt could be seen on his face as he looked at the Messiah making his way up over the lip of the hole of Tartarus. He visibly trembled under the sway of the Messiah's mind link and tried to find a way to play it off. However, those who stood around felt that something was amiss.

The Messiah reached across the void to touch the minds of the inhabitants of paradise. "What is about to unfold is for you to witness as a testimony of conviction!" Then Christ beamed at them.

As Jesus was confronted by Satan and his henchmen, the railing that faced the void was filled with those who had died, expecting the coming of the Messiah.

This would be the picture of all pictures, the teacher thought. "This will be a testimony that will speak louder than ten thousand voices raised in unison, in praise, and they will rise."

The galleries in Hades and in paradise were both full. What was about to happen would be told and retold among themselves for all eternity. John, Adheres, Abraham, and Sarah stood together, joined by Adam and Eve, all wanting to see firsthand the defeat of their mortal enemy, Satan. Jeremiah again chose to be the one to announce the procedure step-by-step. And Abraham thought as he watched, Jeremiah has a knack for bringing clarity and joviality to anything in which he is involved. "I will be watching him in heaven because I just know that he is going to outshout the angels in praise and worship."

"Why are you being insolent, Satan? Do you really think that you have won? Are you that easily fooled? Did you not learn anything in the desert when you tried to beguile me? Where are your manners? You are supposed to kneel to me!"

None of the others in perdition knew what was being said. They were not privy to the ongoing mind meld. On the other hand, those in Abraham's bosom heard the conversation between Christ and the devil.

All Hades residents saw the smug look and slight smile that played around the corners of the Messiah's mouth. On the other hand, the bravado that had been on the face and posture of Satan seemed to have dissipated, leaving him almost mentally naked and in a state of fright mixed with anger. He dropped to his knees, which were literally shaking in weakness. This change in his demeanor and being on his knees did not go unnoticed.

The gatekeeper and Death stood there, seemingly transfixed by the apparition that had appeared over the lip of Tartarus.

"Oh? How? . . . . Ah!" Mephistopheles felt a mental pain unlike any that he had ever experienced. "Come to think of it, I have never felt pain before, except something that I felt when the father decided to boot me out of heaven with Satan. So what is this that I feel? Am I becoming human, feeling every breath inhaled accompanied by a constant degree of pain?"

The gatekeeper was obviously shaken, but while this was a new experience for him, so also was what he saw on the devil's face. Lucifer's whole countenance had undergone a change that was transparent to all who dared to look at him.

"He is kneeling! He is on his knees! It seems like he is trying to fight it! But he is not being successful!" the gatekeeper thought.

Mephistopheles looked at Christ and knew that this was not what the devil or Death had in mind. Everything in that split second of time seemed to have shifted from domination of the devil to submission to the Messiah, who stood calmly a little distance from Tartarus's mouth. Satan had dropped to his knees, visibly shaken and not under his own control.

Again the Messiah touched Satan's mind and asked, "What happened, Lucifer? You seem frozen—no pun intended. You have been mouthing off all night about how you have subjugated me and would make me submit and crawl around on my knees, so why are you not commanding me as you foretold?"

Satan was fighting a physical and mental battle and could not allow himself to respond for fear that he would give way to more of the power that was being exerted on him. "He is supposed to be under my power and authority, but he is not! What gives?" Satan thought.

But Christ knew what he was thinking and smiled even more.

What do I do? Satan thought. "I cannot allow him to come down here and win out over me!" His mind kept turning like a windmill trying to find a solution, but none was forthcoming.

The response from the Messiah was immediate. "Do you think that you can stop me?"

Satan on his knees fell down prostrate before the Messiah. It was a moment in history. There were onlookers; the whole gallery of demons was obviously shaken by what was unfolding before their eyes. They did not know whether to be scared or laugh at the picture which Satan presented—first on his knees, then on his belly.

On the other side, across the void, the whole population yelled joyously. John cried out first with the most intelligible statement of all, "That's it, Messiah. Make him crawl! Make him crawl!"

The demons heard John's voice calling out to the Messiah and looked around to see the whole balcony of paradise lined with onlookers. Then they turned their attention back to the unfolding scene before them. This is all new! one of the demons thought. Another, compelled by some unknown force, uttered the unthinkable statement, "Master Lucifer! Get up on your knees! That is not where you belong!"

Satan flinched under the words of the demon and vowed that he would ring his neck the first opportunity he would have. The statement now drew the attention of the others. Satan and the Messiah were locked in a battle of will, and the devil was losing, not being able to fight back.

Then Christ verbally responded to the encouragement that came from the demon. "You have followed him into rebellion and have suffered for it, yet you have not learned anything."

The demon cringed at the words of the Messiah, acknowledging that he was correct.

"This is what you followed. This is what you gave up wonderful positions in heaven for. It got you nothing but some crawling vermin to be your boss. Besides, you have lost it all for all eternity, with a lot more suffering to come!"

The statement did more to the demon, who now groaned in pain from the truth of the words spoken by Christ.

Satan could not move, no matter how he tried. His mind raced a thousand miles per minute, trying to will himself to stand and face the Messiah in a challenge. But his mind and his legs would have none of it. They would not respond to his mental command. Subsequently, he gave up trying.

Still the Messiah had not once opened his mouth, it made it seem to those observing that the devil was doing it on his own—but not so. Over at Abraham's bosom, souls were privy to the mental onslaught that the Messiah was handing out to Satan.

This is so embarrassing, the devil thought, not wanting to speak out for fear of confirming what he believed the others were thinking.

They had begun to think because Christ had opened their minds to the suggestion that he was controlling Satan's actions. Consequently, they all had this vision of the devil succumbing to the Messiah's wishes. Suddenly Satan spoke, but the words were not of his choice.

"Master! Lord!" The words came from Lucifer's mouth, and he flinched as each word came out along with each breath that he exhaled.

"I will never forget the troubles this demon gave me, and I'm sure that none of you would ever forget either," Jeremiah called out. "Satan seemed to be battling himself about something. He seems to be fighting the urge to kneel before the Messiah, but he is not having any success! There he goes!" And a shout of joy went up from the crowd in paradise, particularly those who were at the dividing rail. Satan dropped to his knees, and this acted as a catalyst for the onlookers in Abraham's bosom. Jeremiah related every syllabus of the scene. The cheers reached the ears of those who stood around Satan encouraging him to get back to his knees. But Satan was having no success in that area. His knees had stopped functioning, and he looked whipped.

Jeremiah, perceiving the crestfallen yet angry figure of Satan on his knees, bellowed with laughter before repeating what was occurring. It did not matter to him that everyone was hearing the same thing that he did; it was a moment that he wanted painted in his heart forever, knowing how the devil had tricked Israel time and again while he was still alive. "This is wonderful!" the prophet said.

And again a cheer went up from the paradise gallery. Christ heard the cheers, as did the devil, and so he said to Satan, "You are making it so easy for me to convict those who have been expecting me for generations that I not to worry that any of them would ever fall into your hands again. You are testifying to them for me, making the father's purpose of salvation for them complete."

The devil's reaction to what was transpiring gave him the courage to force himself to his feet. "You have made a complete fool of me, but I will have the last laugh," he retorted.

"Oh really? And when will that be, Lucifer? You have come up against me and lost every time, so what makes you think that anything will change? Do you not know why I'm here? Oh you will because I will be here for a while yet!"

"No!" Satan shot back. "You will be here forever, Messiah, and I will show you that you should have taken my offering out there in the desert!"

"By the way, your friends in Tartarus, are looking forward to seeing you again," Jesus said.

The devil visibly flinched.

"Touchy, touchy, touchy. You are so afraid of Tartarus while I casually and purposely strode in there and returned. Now what does that tell of you, Lucifer?"

Satan mustered up enough courage to reply. "It tells me that you are getting used to where you will spend eternity. So what do you mean 'a little while longer'? You, sir, are not going anywhere! You are here to stay!"

And the Lord, for the first time, laughed out loudly. His laughter took everyone standing around by surprise. Then he strode off, leaving Satan and his entourage standing there looking befuddled.

That is ridiculous, Satan thought. "To think that I will be there with them at any time! Yes, I encouraged them when they left heaven with me. However, their actions were more than I expected. That is why they are being punished for it. I did not participate in those activities."

"No, you did not, but you were the one responsible for placing the thought in their minds. Therefore, you are the one responsible!"

"This is not the way this day is supposed to start out," Satan said to no one in particular.

As a matter of fact, everyone began ducking into little dark places so that they did not have to face Satan's wrath. But not all of them were quick enough to escape. And so the Messiah strolled off, walking purposely through Hades, while Satan went back to his lair. The crowd at the railing of paradise knew that this was a momentary lull. The Messiah reached across the void to let them know when the next confrontation would occur, and the good crowd looked forward in anticipation.

Christ took leave of the scene at Tartarus's entrance to give himself time to communicate with the father. It was time for him to commune with him, something that he had missed since he was taken to the cross. What's more, Christ was suffering but did not want anyone to have an inkling of it. Furthermore, he missed most this closeness with the father.

"I must recharge myself by connecting with Father. He has promised that if I went into the utter depth of Hades, he would be with me."

"I have not left you or forsaken you, my son. But you know that I cannot help you there because of the agreement that we made!"

"Father, my father!" Christ shouted with joy through all the pain. "Even in Hades you are with me."

"I will be with you always, my son. This is my covenant with you!" Suddenly, all was well with Christ.

"Just hearing your voice is enough encouragement for me to hold on. This is for mankind, and this is for you, my father!"

Jesus walked among those who had not believed, seeking a place to rest, and all fell readily to their knees in acknowledgment. Saul was there, crying about the opportunity that he had wasted. Not wanting the Messiah to see him, Saul tried to hide himself. But there was no place to hide.

"Saul, Saul, why did you choose to disobey my father? Why did you not follow the instructions that I gave you? Now, my people are suffering from that nation that I told you to wipe out. I made you the king of Israel, my chosen people, but you spawned my blessing and my orders for your selfish pleasure. And look what has it got you? This is where your pride and vanity have brought you."

There was nothing, no argument that Saul could make, and so he bowed down on the burning coals of Hades and said, "Master, Lord, God!"

The former leader of Israel wanted to ask for forgiveness but knew that it was too late. Too late, he uttered, as the Messiah walked on. At that moment, he remembered Samuel the prophet whom God had sent to give him directions. The conversation was not lost on Samuel, who often came to the balcony to look from the other side of Hades. And at that moment, Samuel reached out to Saul and said, "Do you remember calling me back from here for your selfish reason, Saul? I remember telling you that you would be here the next day—you and your sons! Now here you are!"

Christ rounded a bend and there stood Cain, the brother of Abel.

"Why, Cain? Why did you slay Abel? He did nothing to you but loved you. You made a mistake, and the father gave you an opportunity to rectify it in your offering. Instead you went out and slew your brother for doing the right thing. Now here you are.

"Did you gain anything from it, Cain? Your father, mother, sisters, and brothers are all over on the other side watching you suffer for your misdeeds. If only you had asked the father for forgiveness, this would not have been your home. It would have ended differently for you. Why?"

"Master, Master!" Cain said, bowing his head in sorrow, remembering and knowing that he could have solved the situation differently. The Messiah walked on by.

Belshazzar saw Christ coming and immediately recognized him. Something in him began to yearn for the teacher's friendship, but he made a mess of things when he chose to have a party with the utensils that were taken from the temple of God.

"What a mess I have made," Belshazzar said.

"You had no respect for my house or the children of my father, Belshazzar. And do not say that you were not warned. After all, your father knew my father. He taught you about him, didn't he? Nebuchadnezzar, your father, spent seven years eating grass until he acknowledged my father, but you learned nothing from it. Why?"

Belshazzar had been thinking this same thing for thousands of years since his demise at the hands of the Medes. But in this one instant, the Messiah brought it all home to him. He hung his head in shame.

The pharaoh, who had enslaved the children of Israel, was crying hysterically as pain contorted his body. He was unaware that the Messiah was standing over him. He looked up and said, "I know you! You have come to torment me more!"

But Christ looked at him with sorrow in his eyes and said, "Far be it from me to do that to you. You had an opportunity to change your mind and let my father's people go, but you chose to try and match wits and strength with him. Moses had warned you; why didn't you believe?"

"I was stupid. I believed that all the intellectuals around me had the answers, but they did not. I should have listened to Moses and Aaron."

"Too late, too late!" the Messiah said and walked on.

The pharaoh crumpled up into the fire in a ball of pain and anguish knowing that his pride had brought him to this point. "I had the opportunity to listen and learn from them, but I was arrogant. I was foolish. Now I pay dearly. Oh! If only I could do it over again."

The pharaoh was shouting to no one, because no one was listening. Some of his Wizards were within hearing of what had just transpired and heard what both had to say. But they too had concerns because they too had been duped by the demons that Satan had sent to influence. They wanted power but did not realize that it would require such high costs. They cried out, not so much because of the fire that consistently burned them as the fact that eternity was a long time to spend in this anguish and pain.

Hades, the Messiah pondered as he strolled along, was full of pain, hurt, disappointment, and disillusion. "This is the result of loving anything other than the father who created all things. Man chose to serve the Creation instead of the Creator. This is the result of their decision. This is a shame. Such an awful waste of soul and spirit!"

Satan tried to keep tabs on him but was unsuccessful. The Messiah moved too fast for the demon that Satan had assigned to keep watch. And so Satan was unaware that he was being viewed from a distance and in a location that he gave no attention to.

None of the demons who had been assigned to Christ could give Satan any accurate information about the Messiah's whereabouts. This bothered him more than it ought to, and he couldn't understand why.

"Master, he was here one minute, and the next he is not. We do not have that kind of power that he demonstrates. We are sorry!"

"That is it," Satan exclaimed. "He has all his powers! But how can that be?"

On the other side of the divide, the saints were waiting with stretched patience for the next assault that was to come. The lookout, Jeremiah, who had been on a constant vigil, kept giving periodic reports to any who would pass by his station.

"That place is a beehive of activities. Everyone seems to be running around, especially since the Messiah gave them the slip . . . I can see Satan becoming angry again. Any time now he is going to lash out at whoever is nearest him. But I see the Messiah: he is standing in a little cul-de-sac off to Satan's right, hiding in plain sight. It seems that the Messiah decided to do just that—hide in plain sight. When the Messiah wants to be found, he will let it happen. Right now, he is hiding in plain sight."

Christ was not hiding from Satan but biding his time according to the father's plan. Christ had retired to speak with the father. It was for this reason that Satan couldn't find him.

Furthermore, Christ was in the throes of pains and recognized that this pain would be the pain that man would have had to bear and would bear if they did not believe that he was Messiah. Thus, he had to do just that—bear the pain until the debt was paid.

The evening of the second day was drawing near, and the time of confrontation between Death, Satan, and Jesus. Christ remained where he was and looked at the destruction that sin had caused, feeling more hurt than any other person in time or space.

Jeremiah watched for any sign of confrontation between the Messiah and Satan and even Death. And as he watched, he realized that a certain melancholy had settled over Jesus.

"Oh Messiah, am I feeling what you are feeling? Or is this empathy that I feel for you in your moment of paying for our sins?"

"You are my servant and friend Jerry," the teacher answered, "so it is only natural that you would feel empathy for me, not for my pain. This is mine alone to bear, but you have that type of heart, as you have shown it for Israel. So thank you for keeping my mind distracted for a moment. However, I must feel, experience, this pain alone. There is no other way to fully pay for mankind's release—no other way!"

Jeremiah felt so helpless in knowing that he could do nothing to assist the Messiah. He then consoled himself with the knowledge that it was only for a short time. "This is temporary. Soon we will see him over here!" The thought cheered him up as he went back to wait for the next confrontation. But none was forthcoming; at least not yet.

"I can see him," Adheres chimed in on Jeremiah's thoughts. "It seems like he is speaking to someone whom I cannot see. If I'm correct, he is talking to the father. He seems to do that a lot! He spoke to him while he was on the cross too. As a matter of fact, at one point the teacher called out and asked the father why he had forsaken him. That troubled me for a while, but then I figured that God did not want to see him like this. I know that I would not want to see my son in such a painful situation, with me not being able to do anything about it. Now that I'm here and things have become clearer, I can understand the father not wanting to see his son suffer the way he did.

"You know, that makes sense to me, John" Adheres continued. "You saw him a lot while you were up there. What do you think? Do you think that he talked to the father a lot?" asked Adheres.

"Oh, we were always far apart from each other except when he came to visit, but I tell you this, I had an experience with him that I will never forget."

Immediately, everyone drew closer. They wanted to hear this experience between John and the Messiah. Ever since the baptist came, everyone had been hanging on to his every word, particularly when the Messiah was mentioned. This occasion was no different.

"What happened?" Joel, one of the minor prophets, asked.

"Oh, that was the first day that he really came to see me," John began. "I recognized him coming and told my disciples that he was the perfect lamb of God. I was shaking in my sandals, just knowing that the Messiah was there in that very place with me! He had always come and stood at the fringes of the crowd that came to see and hear me, but this time was different. I had never thought of mentioning him until that moment!"

"So, what happened," asked Adam, not being able to restrain himself any longer. Everyone knew why: Adam had always felt so guilty that he reached out for any consolation he could find. This story was one of them.

"As he approached me on the embankment of the Jordan River, I saw that there was something about him that exuded power and authority. I actually shook with anticipation for what I did not know. All I knew was that the son of God stood there speaking to me."

"What did he say?" they all chimed in simultaneously.

"I said, 'Master!' Then he said, 'John, I would like you to baptize me.' I was dumbstruck. The Messiah wanted me, a lowly prophet, to baptize him, the son of God the father! I should have been the one to be baptized by him; instead, he asked me to do so for him.

"'Master,' I said, 'I'm not worthy to baptize you!'"

"He asked you to baptize him? Is he that humble to allow himself to be baptized by you?" The question was asked by Joel who stood there transfixed, hearing how the Messiah had humbled himself in this manner. "Well? Did you baptize him?"

"Yes, Joel. I did, but not before he convinced me!"

"And? What happened?"

"What happened afterward was the most interesting and beautiful part."

"Yes, you are just dragging this out and keeping us in suspense." This time the question came from Abraham who was normally conservative, but he now he couldn't hold back.

"I did as he asked, and as he came up from the submersion, the Holy Spirit in the form of a white dove descended from heaven and rested on the Messiah's shoulder. Then out of the skies the voice of God the father spoke, and it was wonderful to hear. He said, 'This is my beloved son with whom I'm well pleased'

"The Messiah was on earth in the flesh, and I had the audacity to be unsure about whom he was."

"Did the people there know what went down there?" someone said. "Does mankind know what the Messiah has done for them? Did they know what kind of commitment he made in that moment of time on the bank of the river Jordan? He gave up all of his glory and riches to come die in our place and give us back spiritual life."

"Brethren, this is what I, we, have been waiting for," said Isaiah, who had pushed his way to the front of the group in time to hear the last part of John's message. "Man's redemption is now paid! We are all now ready to accept him and depart from this place, great as it may be!"

And a shout unrivaled by any previous went up from the group.

John spoke to himself as the shout waned from its tumultuous crescendo, "My job and Adheres's are finished. Now I too can wait for the Messiah to come and rescue us."

Adheres, who was right beside him, said without realizing it, "Amen!"

John looked at him, who looked back, astonished. Both simultaneously repeated "amen," not knowing why.

The crescendo of shouting was not lost on anyone on the other side of the chasm. Every demon, every lost soul, looked up from the drudgery of pain to see what those people were shouting about. But all they could hear was shouting. "Messiah is here! Messiah is here!"

Down in Tartarus, even Judas heard it, and for him, it was a moment of ultimate crisis. "I had it all, and I threw it away for a few measly silver coins that mean nothing to me! I sold out the Messiah. I really sold out the Messiah."

As Judas was saying it, the other occupants joined with him and began mourning afresh as they now knew that their fate was sealed for all eternity.

"What a fool I was!"

Etchers and those who stayed close to him, along with the demon who were given charge over them, had different reactions. The humans, who for some reason stayed close to him, knew now more than ever that the opportunity of their life had slipped through their fingers, never to return, even though they did not know the Messiah. They had heard that he would become a man. They did not believe, and so they now shared hell with those others who likewise did not, or who refused this knowledge of him.

The demon looked confused, trying to understand why the people on the other side were so joyous, why they were claiming that the Messiah had come when he was still over here in a place where no one could leave. As the demons looked at the humans, their confusion became even more profound.

"What do they know that we do not? Is there something that we are missing? Look at them, they actually believe in this Messiah, although he is here! Do they expect him to leave? Hmm . . ."

Death came over and stood by them, trying to make them feel worse, as if they could ever be lower than where they were at that moment.

"Cheer up, gentlemen, because this is for eternity! This Messiah is not going anywhere. He is here to stay!"

When Death said that, the voice that had plagued him before linked to him again.

"Really? Do you really believe that, Death? Have you not learned anything yet? I will leave, and before I do, I will take away your power to do as you please! Do not think that you have gotten off free from punishment. Expect to give an accounting for your part in this whole scheme!"

Death was shaken because he still could not place the voice, clear enough as it was that it was indeed the Messiah talking to him. And the voice said sounded as if it was a threat to which he could look forward.

"I do not understand. I hear a voice but there is no one who seems to have that kind of expertise. So where is it coming from?" Death wondered aloud. "Is it this the Messiah? Na! It cannot be. He is here."

His frustration grew until he wanted to take it out on someone. Unfortunately, Etchers was the only one close enough, and Death lashed out at him physically.

"If you are being smart and playing with my mind, you can expect more of this."

Death was looking over his shoulders, and the fact that he will not die throughout eternity scared them even more.

I should not be afraid of him anymore, Etchers thought. "He cannot kill me a second time. But should I feel again what I have just felt, it may be better if I can just die."

But that was a wish that would never come true for the former thief. His fate was sealed throughout eternity.

"Adheres will live forever, and I will have to endure this death forever." Etchers moaned, and it could be heard even by the Messiah over in the cul-de-sac.

"You chose a rough road to walk, Etcher!"

The end of the second day for the Messiah was fast approaching. He had finished conversing with the father and was ready to take on both Death and Satan one more time.

"I must show them who really is the boss. They do not know whether I'm suffering or not, and I intend to keep it that way."

Christ stepped out of the cul-de-sac. Satan noticed him, and for some reason unknown to himself, Satan wanted to run and hide. He caught himself in time to be reminded that he was in control here in Hades.

"I will not let him have the upper hand anymore—not here where I rule."

The jockeying for dominance started as both eyed each other in the mental war that followed.

The devil spoke loudly for all to hear. "I'm the boss here, and you must do what I ask!"

"So you say," the Messiah retorted, but not verbally.

For that reason, the onlookers of Hades thought that Satan had established his dominance, only to see him drop to his knees in much the same fashion as yesterday. Jeremiah caught the whole scene because he had been looking intently for any such exhibition and was rewarded handsomely.

"They are at it again! Satan has found himself kneeling at the Messiah's feet one more time. Oh, I'm sure that he has conflicting views right now, as to who is the real boss!"

With that comment, everyone was back at the rail looking out at the unfolding scene. Christ simply stood there and watched as the devil dropped to his knees involuntarily.

"You see, Satan, your days are numbered. Do you remember those words you spoke to someone else whom you seduced into an action that cost him his soul? Yes, you do. Well, right back at you, evil one."

Still, the Messiah had not opened his mouth, but all who witnessed this episode and was on hand in yesterday's round realized that more was being played out here than they were seeing or hearing.

None of this was lost on Death, who began wondering when his time would come. Then the Messiah looked at him and smiled, a smile that said more to Death than he wanted to hear. Death cringed without realizing it, and many onlookers knew that Death too was experiencing some of what the devil had been enduring.

"What does he mean that my time will come? That is truly a threat. I, who had him killed and come here. He is saying that my time will come?" A nervous laughter escaped his lips.

Night of the Second Day

Time meant nothing to the Messiah except that which the father had given him to deal with Satan and Death and set the captives of Abraham's bosom free. It was based on this that he orchestrated his time with precision. He was not here to play games with the occupants of Hades but simply to do as was prescribed to him by the father before time began. For this reason, his activities were designed to accomplish three things: conviction, confirmation, and affirmation.

Conviction of the truth had two roles, one of which was to assail those who did not believe in the promise that the father had made or had flaunted them. These were the people and the demons of Hades who were now all around him. With that in mind, everything that he did must send to them a message that was loud and clear—such as who the father was. Not that they did not already know.

"My patience does not mean that I am weak or a pushover," Christ said, beaming at Satan during one of their little mental set to.

Satan now understood only too well that he had no control over his functions when this Messiah was around.

"Oh, so you do understand, or are beginning to understand your predicament, aren't you? Did you think that the father would have allowed you to wreak havoc on his creation and not do something about it? He is simply long-suffering, and this you ought to have known when he slammed you to earth for trying to rise up above him."

Satan remembered well that encounter. He still felt the physical, mental, and spiritual bruises.

Conviction number 2 was the display of hopelessness that these occupants on this side of the divide showed to those on the other side who were watching. This side's conviction would act as a testimony of confirmation and affirmation to them and establish in their minds who he was.

Jesus was confident that John and Adheres had done a wonderful job. Still, what he had to do over here would be the coup de grace to seal their faith and hopes in him. The hopelessness that was displayed here would in turn be the hope of them in paradise. Their faith in the father's word would produce a hope that would soon be realized. Their release was imminent.

Jeremiah was ordained to be the speaker, to give detail of each unfurling event that would act as the catalyst for confirmation and affirmation. The father did think of Jeremiah as the catalyst over there receiving and giving the information as it transpired. Now he could see that the former prophet was doing a wonderful job.

John and Adheres had satisfied their purpose. All that they had to do now was to wait patiently for it all to come together.

Death and Satan were fighting to remember something, but they would not until it was too late. It was wonderful to see them on the receiving end once again. It seemed anytime now Satan would lose it as much as was possible for him to do so.

"Father," Jesus had said, "to think that they had the prophets, from Noah, all the way down to John whom you sent to prepare the way for me. Still they did not believe or accept. The acuteness of this recognition is painful to me! What's more, it acts as a stimulus for the onslaught of pain and anguish for them. I never wanted to see this, Abba, but they had their opportunities to believe that you existed and that you would send a Messiah!

"Still it hurts to know that they will suffer for all eternity. And then there are those who purposely disavow your presence in lieu of Satan now, and they are receiving their just rewards! For these I cannot find any sorrow because they willingly and deliberately chose to serve this evil thing Satan!

"Herod! Do you know me? I'm the one for whom you killed so many babies and young ones, just to assure yourself that you removed me from the scene! Yes, I came as the Messiah to set the captives free. I'm the one for whom you had insecurities, thinking that I came to replace you. You do remember me, don't you? Look across the void, Herod. All of those little ones that you killed are over in Abraham's bosom, waiting for me to take them home to my father, Jehovah God!"

"I know you, Lord. I know you. And when I heard that you were appearing here, at first I was glad, but then I realized that if you are who you are, you are here for a purpose. And when that purpose is accomplished, you will leave.

"Will you forgive me and take me with you?"

"Herod, you were told of my coming to earth to take on the sins of man and set them free. The prophets foretold it, and it was told to you. Thus, your choice to deny or accept and embrace me was yours to make, and you made it. Now it is too late for you. Now you will have all eternity to ponder the choices that you made."

Death was still shaken up from the mental barrage that he endured when the Messiah confronted himself and Satan. He had come to conclude that the teacher was in more control of the situation than Satan. More than him, in fact, even on the issue of his own death.

"We have been manipulated, but why? Did he want to die so that he could come here? Oh, if what I think is true, we are in trouble. I know that something transpired between him and Satan yesterday. His actions proved that. The only person before whom Satan had ever knelt was the father. Yet here he was again, on his knees before the one whom we are supposed to have defeated! Hmm . . . could it be that this Messiah is the father acting as his son?

"Hmm . . . Oh, Satan tried to play it off as if he fell, but he cannot fool me! And today, the same thing occurred again, just as the Messiah stood in front of him. Hmm . . . Something about his countenance and that of the Messiah says differently. Satan knelt before him and couldn't do anything about it. Hmm . . . I have tried to recall something else about Messiah . . . . But . . . I . . . cannot . . . remember! Messiah . . . Ah!

"This frustration is getting to me! I must remember before it is too late, but late for what? Why did I think that? Oh me! I'm getting a bad feeling about this, and that is strange—I'm Death! I do not get bad feelings, I give them!"

Just then, Death heard that voice again speaking in his mind. "There is a first time for everything!"

"What is this? I keep hearing voices? Yet there is no one! There is something strange occurring here in Hades . . . And it all started when the Messiah walked through the gates . . ."

Christ wondered how long before both Death and Satan would come to the realization that Hades as they knew it would not be the same.

"I am here to make drastic changes and to bring to all who inhabit this darkness the realization that their honeymoon is over. It is pitiful that so many humans had fallen under your thumbs, but your time of rejoicing in the dilemma of man has just been shortened in that sense and prolonged to eternity of punishment, demons!

"And when I step through those gates on my way out, it will get even shorter till I return once more. I will be back one more time!"

With that thought, Christ reached out to Death to galvanize him into some type of action.

"Death, what do you think of your actions against those whom I had tried to convict now? Do you still think that you will not have to give an account?"

"Who are you? You keep seeping into my mind like you are liquid, don't you?"

Christ then transferred his thought link to Satan, who seemed to have overcome their last encounter. "Satan, I'm your worst nightmare! Did you not know that I would be here eventually to take back all that you stole? "My father told you that after you tempted Eve and, through her, Adam, you should expect me."

Then Christ turned and walked away, but not before planting a thought in his mind.

Jeremiah, being tuned into what has been occurring in Hades, figured that something was transpiring between Death and Christ, and drew the attention of Abraham.

"Abe, does Death look all right to you? He seems to be in the same predicament as Satan was yesterday. Does it not look that way? See how he seems to become a darker shade of grey!"

"Yes, the Christ has him under some kind of attack! This is great! Hmm, you are right!"

"The Messiah is standing there, not saying anything that can be heard. Yet the reaction of Death makes me think that whatever Christ said to him has got his attention."

"I do not think that the Messiah said anything to him except reach out and touch him in his mind—a little."

"Anyway, whatever is going on between them, Death does not look too good."

Death was rattled, and so was Satan, because nothing seemed to be going the way they had envisioned. Satan began giving the situation some serious thought. Not only did he find himself on the defensive with this son of God. He constantly founds his knees touching the ground as if in submission.

"I tempted him and offered him so much, and he chose to refuse me. Now here he is. He died on that cross. I know because Death saw to it . . . Didn't he? Besides, he is here and no one comes here unless they have died. That is the agreement that I have with the father. So he must have died!

"Too many people saw him die for it not to be a fact . . . . But . . . ahh! Something is wrong!

"I will summon him to my den. And if he refuses, I will go. Hmm, I have not fared so well with him before. And every time I'm before him, I find myself on my knees! I rule . . . Hades!

"I . . . think . . . so.

"Could it be that he did not accept my offer because he knew that he will be here? Na! It cannot be. He did not know that I would have him killed . . . Or did he?

"Daagar! Come in here now!"

"Yes, Lord, here I am. what can I do for you?"

"I want you to find Death, the gatekeeper, Reality, and Reason for me and bring them here now!"

Just as Daagar was about to step into the open, Death walked in. He had been listening to Satan's tirade with himself and knew that he was not the only one who felt that something was wrong.

Furthermore, he also had the urge to come to the lair but did not know why.

"Death, do you think that something may be wrong with this Messiah's presence here? After all, you oversaw his death, didn't you? He did die, didn't he?"

"Yes, Lord, he did die. I saw them lower his body to the ground, wrapped it in burial cloth, and lay him in the tomb. He was dead physically as any man could be. I made sure of that when I prompted one of the soldiers to pierce him on the side with his spear. I saw blood and water gush out with no movement, involuntary or otherwise, from him. No man could have withstood that and not die."

"But Death, he is the son of God. Do you think that maybe he cannot die?"

"Master, to think that is to acknowledge defeat. Besides, when he became human, he gave up that privilege of everlasting life. You and I know that!"

"We think so, but . . ."

No sooner had Satan made that statement than Reality, the gatekeeper, and Confusion walked in.

"Gentlemen! That was quick! You got here so soon!"

"What are you talking about? We were on our way here to see you!"

"What? I sent Daagar to get you all! Something is definitely wrong," Satan fumed. "Death walked in just as I was about to send for him, and now you tell me that you were on your way here even as I sent Daagar to get you!"

"Hmm . . ."

Satan was shaken up and made the most convicting statement that he had ever made. "I feel as if I have lost command of this establishment to him! What do you think?"

"Master! Lord! All of the demons are submissive to you. And every human that died refusing the promise is here under your command. They even do as the demons command! So we say that you have not lost command."

"Do you really believe that, particularly after my last two encounters with him?"

Death had to be very careful not to show what he was really thinking as Satan let loose that tirade. He seems to be slipping, Death thought, but it may be the truth.

"Look at the demons, do you think that they still respect me after seeing me on my knees before him?"

"Hmm, so Christ really did not have a choice in the matter. My suspicions are confirmed!" Death thought.

"You only have to be more cruel to them. If they have any intention of being disobedient because they think that you have lost, that would change immediately!"

"Yes! I can regain my standing in this matter, to have control whether he is here or not!"

The questions that Satan had put forth were rhetorical, of course, not really looking for an answer. Besides, no one would have wanted to take a chance on answering him if he was looking for an answer.

Reason walked in. He did not want to be first for this meeting because he had seen Satan on his knees and knew that it really made him mad. A mad Satan is a dangerous Satan.

Satan turned and looked at him. "You are late, Reason. Where have you been?"

"Why do you ask? Did you send for me?"

"Of course, I did. I sent Daagar to get you all."

"I did not see him, and I do not know. I just had the urge to be here. "Can anyone tell me what is it that I'm missing about this man Christ?"

The silence in the room was pregnant because they had no answer; at least none that would suffice.

"Master," says Death, "ever since he walked through the gates, I have had a sinking feeling in my stomach. I cannot for the life, er, death, of me identify the reason, but I do know that there is something that we are missing. It is vital information, but it keeps eluding my consciousness,"

"Does anyone feel the same way or is this just a premonition?" Satan asked.

When there was no forthcoming answer, he said, "Well, I too have had those feelings. However, I cannot recall the reason why. So maybe Reason can give us some idea about it!"

Reason was hoping that the conversation would not directly involve him because what he had to say may not sit well with Satan.

"Master, I have given what you are saying some thought and have formed an idea about it all. Remember that I have not been privy to these misgivings that seemed to have permeated the enclave. However—"

That was as far as he got when he was rudely interrupted. Everyone in the room jumped as if burnt by fire too.

"You are weak and selfish. You have destroyed what the father has built. Your pride has brought you to this place, and here you will stay."

"You had the audacity to come to me to bribe me while I'm about my father's business, and for this I will come back and sentence you to Tartarus that you so fervently avoid. But I promise you that you will have company in your misery."

No one knew that Christ, the Messiah, had been in the room. They were taken aback by his slew of words. These were the first words that Christ had verbally spoken to any of the demons and Satan.

"So, you speak! You will not infringe my mind again!" Satan was flustered as he spoke. "How did you get in here without my permission anyway?"

"I do not need your permission, Satan. This you should have known ever since the father created you. It does not matter that this is your dominion because you are still under my command. Moreover, my father told you to expect this."

"Yes, that is it! I couldn't remember what it was that was lurking in the shadows of my mind. But now I can see it," said Death.

What the group did not know was that the Messiah had come in at the moment Death also walked in. He had intended on attacking

Death once more but considered this meeting more important. Besides, he had opened the ears and eyes of every person in Abraham's bosom to see and hear what transpired in the room. They were seen and heard as a confirmation to the occupants of paradise. And so arose a joyous burst of shouting from across the way.

Those, who resided in this part of Hades felt even more depressed at the joy that their counterpart displayed. Each time it occurred, the joy of the paradise people resounded and went up by octaves. Their Hades counterparts' sorrow, on the other hand, became more acute, causing them deeper depression.

Satan jumped to his feet and asked, "Why are they shouting over there? It is as if they are privy to what is transpiring here?" And as soon as he said it, another shout of joy went up in paradise. Satan was dumfounded.

"Are they hearing this and all of the other things that have been going on here?"

"Yes," Christ answered.

"How? Who is the cause of this?"

"I caused it," Christ responded. "I'm the only begotten son of God, Satan. I can do anything, but I now do only what the father tells me!"

"Then you are saying that you have acted under the instructions of the father?"

"Yes! Do you have a problem with that?"

Satan was visibly shaken. He had never considered that the father would intrude into his lair. Secondly, he did not realize how much power this Messiah had. Right then and there, he knew that he was in for an extended problem.

I should not have had him killed . . . maybe this unfolding situation would not have occurred, Satan thought. He soon realized that Christ read everything that was in his mind.

Christ smiled ruefully and said, "You had no choice, Satan. The cost of retrieving mankind from your power had to be paid, and I was the one chosen to pay it. Eternity is extended for you, Satan."

Lucifer jumped involuntarily because again Christ spoke but only into his mind. Everyone in the room wondered why he jumped so suddenly, but the look on his face gave the indication as to what had happened. And so the devil's thoughts began to search for reasons that were not forthcoming. At least to him, it seemed his mind was being held ransom by the Messiah.

"This is your future prison, so you should get used to it. Those friends of yours in Tartarus will be expecting you."

Satan screamed with a loud voice that really got the attention of everyone in Hades and in paradise. He had never thought that Tartarus would be his portion, and now he knew! Satan, while sitting there in his lair, felt pain as he had never felt it before. It was painful beyond his imagination.

"This is where you will spend eternity Satan, you and a great number of your friends here! Some will be coming alone in the future and will be your guests for eternity. I just wanted you to know that since you lost the battle on Calvary when you chose to have me killed. But, there is more to come. I will give you a peek into your future!

"Look! Do you know that man? You seduced him into killing six million Jews. How about that one? His name is Genghis Khan. Of course, you know him. He is down there right now.

"How about him—he is the anti-Christ? But of course, you know him also, do you not? Would you like me to go on?"

Satan screamed even more because the pain was the pain of eternity, locked in and cannot leave.

"Fire . . . intense . . . fire!"

Christ had been in more pain ever since he went through the gates of Hades. However, Satan and his demons were unaware of it. Jesus gathered his strength from the shouting that erupted into the air periodically.

It worked like an aphrodisiac, a stimulant to his system, and gave the Messiah the strength to continue. However, the devil was not aware of it. Christ had already decided that it was a small price to pay for the redemption of mankind. And now the end is near. Soon he will be leaving this place, having paid the ransom required to set humanity free from sin.

Nothing was lost on the members of paradise. Christ came to earth to suffer; he bled and died. This also included coming into

Hades and continuing the mandate that was laid out before time began. Jesus had to feel what humans would feel if they, instead of him, were in Hades. For that reason, even in Hades he suffered, although unknown to the devil and his associates.

However, those who are on the other side of the void—paradise—knew what he was feeling because they were tuned in to him. In other words, they felt for him, knowing that he was suffering as they would have, if they were not people who believed in the Messiah's coming!

It was all worth it, Jesus kept reminding himself. Every time he heard the shouts of joy coming from the other side, he knew that his task was coming to a conclusion. He had never doubted the father, not even for a nanosecond.

The Messiah's pain was rewarded by the reaction of Satan and Death on the one side and by the joy that emanated from the other. Both were a balance for him to steady him to persevere. It was only for a while, not eternity, and that was gratifying. Soon, very soon, he would take his leave of this place—all its pain and suffering—and join his friends who have waited for his coming for centuries; some, in fact, for thousands of years.

Satan's voice brought Christ back to the reality of Hades when the devil asked, "What have I done that deserves such a treatment from you and the father?"

"You asked that question, Satan? "Look around you, at all the suffering and pain that you have brought to his creation. Look at the number of people that you have deceived into thinking that there is no God or the people that you have caused to worship creation instead of the Creator! Look, Satan, look at your testimony!

"Look at those whom you have caused to curse the father and die. Look at those who followed in folly you out of heaven. Look at your handiwork, Satan.

"Your pride caused all of this, and your pride is now the instrument of your pending demise. Do you really think that the father could forgive the havoc that you have caused in his creation, which does not have the attitude of repentance?

"I think not! Many have joined you in your deceit, and many more will join you. They, as you have taught them, will take the line of least resistance for a few measly pieces of silver, gold, emeralds, and diamonds, not knowing that the father had intended them to have them in the first place. Oh no, Satan, your punishment has only begun."

Satan screamed loudly. Christ had mentally placed him in a situation where he thought that he was still in Tartarus, among those that he had guided into an evil path. It felt so real that he screamed in agony from the sins that beset the residents of that place. His state was such that it was witnessed by everyone in that room—those over at the railing of Abraham's bosom and to all in perdition. They knew that it was he, Satan, who screamed. When Christ again touched his mind, bringing him back into the lair, he was frightened into a paleness that was unlike him.

"You see now, Lucifer? Do you now understand how your past, your present as well as your future will be? Hmm . . ."

Christ then turned his attention to Death and said, "It is your turn, Death!"

Everyone in the room became pale, thinking that they would also be a part of this punishment being meted out.

"Lord, what have I done that requires this punishment?" Death asked. "I simply followed the outline that was laid out for me!"

"You enjoyed your work too much, Death!"

"Remember me while I was on the cross? What were you doing then? Were you sympathetic to me? Did you feel any kind of remorse? No! You stood there in the throes of ecstasy, watching me suffer! I'm the only begotten son of the father, and when you hurt me, you also hurt him!"

Death's response was instinctive. "We did not know that; at least I did not know that! It was never my intent to hurt you!"

"But you did," the Messiah replied. "And you enjoyed it, sadistic evil!"

Death winced as he felt Christ's mental power assail him mentally. So this is what Satan felt, he thought as the onslaught on him began.

"Yes Death, this is what he felt and will always feel from this point onward. It will cause him to lash out and the residents of this place to want to overthrow him. And you will not be in any better position, Death. You will always contend with them and those who confess me.

"You will find that you have no more authority over them. They will welcome you when they have decided to come home to me. But that is all that you will be able to do—nothing more! Simply assist them to cross over into my arms as I wait for them. And it will hurt you more than you can now imagine.

"As a matter of fact, let us go on a little journey into the future, shall we?"

Death's countenance, which had always been a pale grey, now changed as he mentally felt pain that was foreign to him previously.

"Oh! Messiah! Please, have mercy on me!

"Ah! How could this be? They are in the lion's den being killed and relishing their deaths! That is not possible! It is as if I have no effect on them! The pain, the pain! Stop it. This is no fun!"

"Ha! No fun, you say. Just as you had fun at my expense, so you will not have fun from their deaths, and that will be the pain that you will endure! Then will come that time when you and your host, Satan, will be thrown into Tartarus among your associates who look forward to that moment in time!"

"Time, did you say time? Why are we to be subjected to time?"

"The answer is simple, you will know what time means to those humans who will be here with you throughout eternity. Then you will understand what it is to live for an eternity of time with pain, ever-increasing pain!"

As Christ made that last statement, he released Death from the mental agony that he was experiencing.

"What do you want from us?" It was a simultaneous question from him and Satan.

The confrontation continued until Satan was also a bundle of emotions running wild. The Messiah, notwithstanding the pain that he was feeling, enjoyed every moment of discomfort that the devil and Death experienced. This fact was not lost on the onlookers in paradise. Neither was it lost on the souls who were now trapped in punishment for all eternity.

Through their pain and suffering, they saw through the person who had caused their demise and were appalled that they had allowed him to do this to them. Christ then said to Satan and Death, "Things are changing for both of you very much; the power that you once wielded down here will soon evaporate. Then it will be interesting to see what happens after that."

Just then, Christ heard the voice of his father saying to him, "You have suffered enough, my son. From this point on, the pain will be nonexistent, so go about your business of doing my will with more freedom."

Instantaneously, a joyous shout arose on the other side. Christ knew then that they too knew—he was free. He had come through for mankind. The debt had been paid in full. Now he can consolidate his efforts here in Hades and be gone when the time was right.

Satan saw the change, as did Death, and realized for the first time that Christ had been suffering all along.

"You did not let us know that you were suffering," Satan wheezed as he now writhed in pain. "You were feeling pain and never allowed us to see it!"

"That is correct, Satan. I could not allow you to see until it was over. It was the price that I had to pay for the redemption of mankind. You and Death exacted a great payment for the return of the father's flock. And I came to make that payment for them, to return them to where they belong."

Rage took hold of Satan at that moment and would not let him go.

"Now that it is almost done, you may know, as you ought to, that my father, his holy spirit, and I implemented this plan of redemption in which you participated, thinking that in my death you both won. You did not know, but we did! You have lost, Satan.

"Man's redemption is truly paid in full. No longer do they have to worry, if they accept my contribution, my grace, my sacrifice for them. No longer do they have to kill animals, birds, and other living things so that the blood can be a temporary measure of forgiveness for them. They have just witnessed the only blood sacrifice that they ever have to make to be free of you forever."

Satan groaned. He had thought that he won, but now the reality of the situation became evident. He looked up at those who were looking down at him and saw revilement, despicable hatred, and contempt. He knew that he had sunken to a new low.

Thus, the Christ remarked, "You are enjoying this, aren't you Satan? Yes! You have caused so much pain and suffering that I and those who have been victimized by you should be allowed an opportunity of respite by seeing you on the receiving end. And every pain that you suffer gives rise to the satisfaction that is felt in paradise and the eternity of hurt that these over here will suffer with you."

"I'm seeing a side of you that you did not exhibit before," Satan responded.

"And here is another bit of information that you may savor for all eternity," Jesus went on. "Anyone who confesses me as the only begotten son of the father from this moment on is out of your reach. No matter how much you tempt them, and no matter how they sin, they simply have to remember that my blood shed on Calvary and in Pilate's praetorium, automatically cleanses them and frees them for all eternity!"

It was close to evening of the second day, and Christ knew that it was time to take his leave of hell and its occupants. Satan at that moment realized that something was up, that the Messiah was about to do something spectacular but did not know what it was.

"Are you about to leave us?" The question involuntarily came from Satan.

"Why, yes, now that you mentioned it. But before I go, I want to let you know that in losing to me, you and Death have relinquished your authority of hell to me! And you, Death, you will now find that your authority over me is also now relinquished to me!"

The Messiah then turned and headed out of the lair, the occupants streaming out behind him. No one had ever left hell once those gates were closed behind them. Thus, the gatekeeper smiled with a knowing grin.

"We will see about that! Those gates only open to let people in, not out. So I do not think this Messiah is going anywhere!"

Satan and Death drew some courage from Mephistopheles' words but felt that it might not be as he had said. The Messiah strode confidently toward the gates, having read their thoughts and heard the gatekeeper's confident analysis.

On his way out of Satan's den, the Messiah stopped, turned around, and looked at the two dejected individuals standing in the doorway of darkened room. The joy that they had expected to celebrate was premature. They now knew it. The teacher smiled and said to himself, This is the first real pleasure that I have had in this evil place!" The look on his opponents' faces was enough to bring joy to his heart. Then he spoke out loud, "What you are experiencing now is nothing compared to what is yet to come!"

Satan cringed involuntarily at the remark, as if somehow the future had touched him and it was not good. Christ spoke words that cut into the very heart of Satan and Death.

"O Death, where is your sting? How come I'm free to walk away from you undaunted? Where is the power that you thought you had over me? I'm about to leave, and there is nothing that you can do to stop me!"

As he made that statement, a cry rose up on the other side—in Abraham's bosom—because those words meant that he was victorious. "The teacher, the Messiah, will soon be here now!" a number of them said in unison as they heard the words spoken to Death.

"O Hades, where is your victory?"

These words were really intended for the devil and all of Hades, who believed that they would have Christ among them for all eternity. But it was not to be, and it became even more apparent when he asked Satan that question, although he referred to Hades. What they had thought was not going to be because the Messiah was about to take his leave of the area.

"Hades, you could not hold me, and I have done what the father has asked of me! I can now rejoice and all heaven is rejoicing even as I speak! It is a joyful noise, Satan, one that you would not be able to relish! I'm victorious!"

He turned and strode toward the door and the gates of Hades!

All eyes, those of Abraham's bosom and those of the residents of perdition, were on Christ and the gates.

"What will happen," one of the humans by the side of the path asked to no one in particular.

Etchers, who was nearby, said, "Maybe we should follow him. If the gates open, we will leave with him."

And so they flooded the path behind the Messiah, hoping that he would lead them free from torment. But it was not to be. As Christ came closer to the gates, the gatekeeper smiled because the gates did not budge. However, there was no slowing in the teacher's walk.

Christ knew that everything he did and said on this side of perdition was designed by the father to convict, confirm, and affirm those on the other side of the void. What transpired between him and the occupants of perdition did also register on those who were given access to hear and understand, as the father had opened their eyes and ears to see and hear.

John the Baptist, as he was fondly called by his friends and neighbors over in Abraham's bosom, was not aware of what transpired after he died at the request of the king. Thus, he was unaware that Judas had sold out the Messiah to the high priests. When he heard it, Adheres, knowing that Judas was one of the Messiah's disciples, was troubled. When he saw Judas head toward the pit behind Christ, he had a sense of relief, knowing that he was true to the commission that the father had given him.

Abraham, who happened to be looking at him while the story unfolded between Judas and Christ all the way to Tartarus, had seen John's reaction and wondered. But in wondering, Abraham spoke his thoughts out for all to hear, including John.

"He is wondering if any of his apostles did the same thing to him. I can see from his face that he is troubled."

John, hearing him say it, turned and inquired if he was referring to him. Abraham answered, "Yes! You gave me the impression that it grieved you that one or more of your apostles might have done it."

"Yes, it did cross my mind!"

"I can see how that would bother you, particularly after being placed in prison and beheaded."

"Abe, do you think that they may have done this too?"

"No, I do not!"

And John left it at that but thought of asking the Messiah his thoughts on it when he came.

Time moved along slowly for those who found themselves in the grip of hopelessness. However, it was no different for those on the other side of the void. For them, time moved too slowly for them because they lived in anticipation of redemption, freedom which could only be given through the Messiah. For them time's slowness had a different meaning compared to those who faced the hopelessness of eternity in Hades. Whereas, for them it was temporary, in Hades it was permanent. The residents of Hades was now permanent, but the residents of paradise had a much better place to look forward to—heaven. All things being equal, both had a stake in seeing time go by faster.

The consolation of the residents of paradise was the coming of the Messiah—Christ. Every moment of waiting was like a needle of anxiety pricking their consciousness. The waiting was an anguish, not exactly like pain but with some of its effect.

Waiting could sometimes be painful. It was not the type of pain that those on the other side experienced, but it was somehow the same pain of waiting, the impatience of knowing that soon it would be unspeakable joy and full of glory—the Messiah would soon be here. Majority of the population in paradise had been waiting for thousands of years for this occasion.

It was hard to control the emotions that ran through the community. Simply thinking about it brought waves of joy. Having to wait brought an impatience that was thinly veiled, suppressed, kept under control. It was a monumental task for everyone but more so for such people as Noah, his sons and daughters and, before them, Melchizedek, Abel, Enosh, Seth, and many others who had known of his coming.

There was a feverish pitch of tenseness that permeated paradise because all that they could think of was "the Messiah will soon be here" or "the Messiah is on the other side and preparing to come to us." During the revelry, someone said, "Save the best for last, and we are the last!" A cheer went up that resounded with the joy which sparked. Suddenly, everyone was chanting, "They are first, we are last! Haha!"

That day marked the closing time, the evening of the second day of Christ in Hades. The people rejoiced with wild abandon.

King David rounded up men and women with trumpets, violins, timbrels, and harps and started a dance that rivaled the one he did before his wife on the streets of Jerusalem. All of paradise was dancing, and it took away the anguish of waiting for the Messiah.

Christ on the other side felt the anxiety that pervaded paradise and was glad when David thought this up. The party was in full swing. The third day was fast approaching, and everyone knew it. Christ had in Hades for two nights and two days. Soon it would time for his appearance in paradise, and that was the momentous occasion that they all waited for.

"Where is Eve?" Adam asked.

"The same place where Sarah is," Abraham answered.

"And where is that, Brother Abe?" Adam responded.

"You know, you are the first man, but you do not have a clue about women," Abraham responded.

Adam's sheepish grin at the remark showed that he was in the dark, but more important, Abraham was sorry that he mentioned it.

It was not designed to provoke Adam's memory of what transpired to cause all of this, but it did. And it could be seen by the fleeting touch of pain that went quickly across Adam's eyes and face. Adam was still sensitive about eating the fruit given to him by Eve, knowing that it was that incident which had led all mankind down this path of redemption. Abraham knew that he had to cheer Adam up and wracked his brain to find a way. It came to him.

"Adam, please sit here a while with me. We have to talk before the Messiah gets here.

"Know this," Abraham consoled the first man, "if you had not eaten that fruit, we would not be celebrating now! It is a joy to know that we are overcomers. It is wonderful to know that we have grown to this point and its subsequent satisfaction. Do you not think that the father knew this would happen? Do you not think that he knew that Satan would have tried?"

"Yes!"

God knew that Satan would succeed, and that it was an opportunity for man to grow to the maturity that God desired. We are his children, and if he wanted to stop it, he only had to think about it, and Satan would have eaten grass, being put so low on his belly. So give God some credit, will you?"

"Adam, do you really think so?"

"Look around you. Don't you think that the father is rejoicing with us? "Having known and spoken to him, I'm sure that he is enjoying every moment of this. It is what he lives for. It is what he created us for!"

Adam was somewhat relieved by Abraham's summation. On the other hand, Abraham was saying under his breath, "Father, I do not presume to know as you know, but I had to say something to cheer him up. Please forgive me!"

At that moment, he heard Christ laughing in his mind, and Abraham knew that Christ had heard the whole thing!

"Messiah! It is good to feel your presence again. So how much longer, Lord? Lord, how much longer do we have to wait?"

"Not long, Abe. Abe!"

"Yes, Lord?

"Oh, I rather enjoy that little nickname that they have pinned on you!"

"May I say 'funny,' Lord?"

"You already have! The moment you thought about it, you said it!"

"Forgive me, Messiah. It was not intended to be negative."

"I did not take it as negative, Abe. In fact, we will be having wonderful conversations like this for all eternity! Now how does that grab you?"

Eve and Sarah walked into sight and immediately drew the attention of their husbands. All of Adam's anxiety fled when he saw the first woman.

"Eve!" Adam said. "You have not lost it. It is still there! Wow!"

Abraham, not to be outdone, took one look at Sarah and was choked at the sight that he beheld. "Woman, age has nothing to do with you. It has stood aside and let you through unscathed. Wow!"

Everyone in paradise wanted to see these two beautiful women whom God had made and given to their fathers. They were stupendously gorgeous and resplendent. Adam and Abraham knew that their lives had been blessed by God for giving them their respective mates. Of course, this caused all the females of paradise to join in, in preparation for the Messiah.

Christ looked across the void at these two women and stated without reserve, "You are both truly the work of my father. He placed in each of you a beauty that cannot be duplicated. Your uniqueness is his blessing and joy, and I speak for him in this. Prepare because I'm coming to the celebration soon.

"I have only one more thing to do over here; then you can see me in person. I have only to command the gate, and I will be there!"

Christ walked up to the gates and said, "Open!"

The gates automatically swung outward, as if to flee his presence.

"Oh! Hey! Oh come on, gates! What is this?" The words escaped from Mephistopheles' lips. "This has never happened before! So why is it happening now?"

"Don't you understand, Meph? I now own the keys to this place! I now have the final say, not you, not Death and, definitely, not Satan! Me! I'm the one who has the final say!"

Those who followed tried to get through, particularly Etchers, but the gates would not allow any other human through to the outside. Etchers screamed and said, "So close yet so far away!"

The Messiah turned to Satan just before leaving Hades and said to him, "I am the Second Adam, Satan!" And Christ walked through the gates of hell.

> And the angels who did not keep their proper
> domain but left their own abode, He has reserved in

everlasting chains under darkness for the judgment of the great day; as Sodom and Gomorrah and the cities around them in a similar manner to these, having given themselves over to sexual immorality and gone after strange flesh, are set forth as an example, suffering the vengeance of eternal fire.[14]

The Messiah's Entrance into Paradise

Wonderful! Marvelous! Stupendous! All these superlatives could not adequately describe what the Messiah saw as he traversed the void and came closer to this wonderful place. As a man, he had never seen it, but as God's son, he was the architect of it. He was looking at it for the first time through the eyes of a man, and it was awesome.

Yet as Christ, knowing that he, the Spoken Word, spoke it into existence, it gave him a sense of joy and happiness. "Mankind is worth this! It is worth knowing that the devil could not touch them as they waited for my coming, and the moment is here! My father, you outdid yourself here! Your plan for man's redemption worked perfectly, and the devil was none the wiser for it. He had no clue that this place was as beautiful and joyous as it is. Happiness, joy, and peace have existed here for thousands of years and can be seen even in the atmosphere.

"No wonder that Satan and his henchmen could not—did not—know how to get in. They would have brought something that should not have been here in the first place. This is the masterpiece, Father, and it is what you wanted the Garden of Eden to look like for all times. Tall oak trees, spiraling toward heaven, as if in an attempt to touch God's hand. Junior Oakwood, you would have been proud to be here and see these! The cedars are more beautiful than those of Lebanon."

Everything is so immaculate, thought Christ as he approached the rail. "Blessing and beauty hand in hand hold up this place before the father as the residents of this little part of heaven give glory to him. They anticipate my coming to release them for their final journey—heaven!"

The difference between Hades and paradise was significant. Hades was full of the stench of burning flesh and worms that would not die. The worms were destructive yet not destroying because nothing in Hades could be destroyed. Evil permeated every crevice of that place. On the other hand, in paradise joy, happiness, and righteousness held counsel. The pains that the worms and evil caused as they infiltrated the bodies of the human occupants of yonder Hades were missing here.

The comparison is astounding, Christ thought. "And rightly so! The punishment for sin is death, eternal death. Not dead but feeling everything as if they are alive. The residents of Hades feel everything that happens to them even more so than when they were alive physically. And this they must bear until the end of eternity!

"Adam must have had a hard time dealing with this paradise, having failed in his last assignment. But as the second Adam, I came to set it right and give him peace. Now it is done, his—their—redemption is paid in full, and they can now fully enjoy all that the father has prepared for them."

All these Christ was thinking about as he approached paradise.

"I want to savor this change, this reality, having had the displeasure of being on the other side and hurting for mankind. Yes, I did hurt—a lot—as part of my payment for mankind's sin. I had to endure all that they would if they did not accept me as my father's only begotten son. Thus, my pain and anguish had to be the same as theirs. Now it is over, with only one more thing to do, which I look forward to doing.

"Father, I thank you for the strength to do what was required of me in Hades. I now have the keys to Hades and the grave. I have defeated the devil and neutralized his power over those who from this day forth will believe in me as your begotten son. Now I go to offer myself as the door for those who have waited for me to come.

"Even in death they waited—from the first man and woman—to this moment. I have kept them all, except for Judas Iscariot! And even him I tried to save him, but he could not be saved. Satan had won him over, and kept him in bondage by guilt!

"I can hear the wailing of anguish and pain behind my back. Pain and suffering are having the time of their lives over there!

Satan's anger will be demonstrated more now than before. He knows now that he has lost, and that it is only a matter of time before the completion of his judgment is announced.

"I look forward to that. He will have his last fling—he and Death—but it will come to an end soon. Mankind is now free to make their choice again, to love and serve my father as they believe that I am the Christ sent by the father. Or they can continue in the sin in which they were born and shaped.

"Whereas, they saw only the law and its perfection, they can now see grace through me and know that they can have a better ending to their physical, mental, and spiritual being.

"Adam and Eve have been avenged! Now they can live and know that mankind is now saved for all eternity. I can feel his impatience and pain o the knowledge that he has been the cause of all this. However, we, the Triune, knew that it would happen and was prepared for it. Now we let Adam off the hook, Father.

"Eve has been silent, but I know how she feels. I know that, more than Adam, she feels bad for having introduced the fruit to him and forcing him to choose her instead of choosing the father. How often has she wanted to tell Adam that but did not because of the pain that he constantly carried! Now mankind is back to square one, to choose as they see fit.

"Mankind has to love us of their own accord. It is the only way that true love can function. It cannot be coerced or bought. It must be given freely to us, as we have done. This is the format that I know my father wanted, and the Holy Spirit and I will not deviate from it. Thus, the few that love us are the ones that we want for all eternity.

"Adam and I will talk. I'm sure that the conversation will enlighten him more than any other. Abraham's conversation should have done it, but the guilt that he carries still is a bother to him. I can feel it. He and Eve are practically in a Hades of their own!"

The nearer the Messiah got to paradise, the more he thought of the things that he should do.

Paradise is a place or state of ideal beauty, loveliness, or rapture. Rapture is a state or expression of ecstasy. Ecstasy is intense joy or delight. Mere words cannot describe this ideal place. Man living on earth cannot fathom the beauty that encompasses this place. Men may write about it but have nothing to compare it to.

"Love, true love, bathes the air with a fragrance that cannot be explained in mere words as it takes on a whole new meaning, a heavenly meaning. And this is the way everything ought to be," Christ reflected.

"Mankind deserves the best, having been made in the father's image. This was and is his intent! So, Satan and Death, I say now, remember, your judgment is at hand!"

Christ's introspection took hold of him and wrapped itself around him like a blanket. A wonderfully woven blanket, he thought.

"If living man could experience this lifestyle, they would be raised up to the level of angels with more feeling for beauty. They would be able to appreciate having a soul and body that feel, experience, and react. Man's body, intricately made of flesh, is well built by the father Satan has defiled.

"I will make sure that his days in eternity never cease to be full of pain. My father gave me this wonderful opportunity to experience it, and it is wonderful. It is majestic! But man does not know it! Man does not know it. How unfortunate!"

Two groups of people watched the Messiah leave Hades. For one group, it was the last ray of hope petering out into utter darkness. For the other, it represented hope beyond hope. Judas Iscariot watched his hope for salvation diminish over the rim of Tartarus. Etcher, stopped by an impenetrable barrier, watched as he who was hope walked through the gate of Hades. It was the end of hope, as Etchers now knew it.

Many others came and joined the former thief. They gazed at the Messiah's receding form. Each person had questions for themselves, not to ask any other person but to their choice of paths. There was Jezebel, for instance, who had wanted to kill Elijah for having slain the priests of Baal.

"I did not believe that there would be a Messiah. I often heard the Israelites talk of him, but I thought it was a myth. Oh how wrong I was. Now here I am, and I had to hide so that he could not see me!"

"You are wrong, Jezebel. I saw you and Ahab, your husband. I saw your actions trying to hide in plain sight. But I decided not to torment you. I was not there to bring you or the other resident companions any pain but to drop off the sins and curses of those who believed."

King Saul was also there, locked into his own thoughts as usual, still trying to figure out his problem. He could not understand why he ended in Hades. Christ decided to tell him, knowing that he did not realize that Christ would reach across the gulf and touch his mind.

"Saul, your sin was your pride. You were narcissistic, thinking selfishly and not caring about the people that my father placed under your authority. You took advantage of them and tried to slay the servant of my father! You tried to kill David, whom the father had anointed to supercede you. Notwithstanding that your son and he had formed a bond of brotherhood, you still wanted David dead.

"Moreover, Saul, you went and became involved with one thing that my father detested among many things. You were involved with sorcery, Saul. To wit, you had that woman call Samuel from paradise to try to fix your problem after the fact.

"My father would have forgiven you, if you had only called on him, but your pride did not allow you. You became even more selfish in your actions and discounted the information that Samuel gave you. For in those instructions was your salvation! But you did not heed to them. So here you are today!"

Herod, the great procurator of Israel, was there. He was the one who wanted Christ dead. He had killed all the male children who were of Christ's age bracket. In Hades he had tried not to let Christ see him, but Christ did and said to him, "Herod, all the young male Israelites that you killed in the process of trying to annihilate me are over on the other side. God forgave them of their sins because they were too young to understand. But they now know of you and what you did!"

"I guess that this is my payment for that?"

"You said it, and it is for all eternity."

Silently, Herod wondered, What would have happened if I had killed him?

"You will never know, Herod." Christ beamed at him.

"What? You can speak to me from a distance? You can scarcely be seen from here!"

"Even if I was a million miles away, I would still hear you breathe, speak, and think, Herod. Nothing is hidden from me it all comes to me!"

Herod flinched as he felt the voice of Christ in his mind. All he could think of was "I tried to kill him!"

Cain saw Christ go and thought that if he had not killed his brother Abel, he would probably be on the other side right now waiting for the Messiah to come.

"I allowed the devil to overcome me, and here I now stay with him for all eternity. I simply blew it. I should have asked the father's forgiveness. I would not be in this predicament now! And here is my whole family, my whole line wiped out so that we could not enjoy the world. Why didn't I rethink the way I did things then? I would not have been here now!"

He began to be in distress anew. Christ wanted to reach out to console him but thought better of it. Cain's pain and anguish became more intense as he moved his body involuntarily. As he tried to stay silent and unmoving, he heard a voice say to his mind, "That is how Abel felt."

On the other side, there was a full contingent waiting for him. Christ felt the pent-up energy seeping into the atmosphere which surrounded paradise.

"This is a living thing," he said. "Life coming from life as the father meant it to be. The joy of life is really living it the way my father had intended, and these people are about to enjoy it even more than they now do. The beginning of the end is here, and the beginning of another beginning also approaches.

"I bear my wounds gladly to make this happen and to see its fruition. This is indeed a wonderful day. And it has not even begun to be as wonderful as it will get."

The inhabitants of paradise lined the avenue along the rail from which they periodically looked out at Hades. The fires seemed to be raging more now than before. Thus, they wondered what the Messiah had done that may have caused it.

Adam was thinking of Cain, as was Eve. There in that awful place resided their first child. Satan took him from them. Cain was a constant part of their thoughts.

Adam, more than any other person, thought that it was ironic Satan took his firstborn as if as payment for something. It was the devil who deceived them; it was the devil who owed them. These were his thoughts when Christ reached out and stopped him from punishing himself so unnecessarily.

"Time to let go of that, Adam. You were made unhappy by Satan not because he disliked you but because he hated the father. Now that situation is corrected, and you are back on the path that the father planned for you. So let go of it now!"

The first Adam felt in his mind the soothing touch of the second Adam and turned to look at Eve with a wistful smile playing on the corners of his mouth.

"The second Adam, your offspring, comes to save us, Eve darling, just as he said he would."

"I'm happy now to see the damage that we caused rectified."

Eve looked up at Adam with all the pain a penitent mother could bring forth and wept through the words that she spoke next. "Adam, I'm so sorry for all of this. Please forgive me!"

Jesus, about to make his grand entrance, came to a stand still. All the forgiveness ever mentioned in the world did not have as much import as the one he had just picked from Eve. It made him stop to regain his composure.

"After all, I'm still a human spirit until my father puts me back into that body lying in Joseph's tomb. This just made it all worthwhile."

A smile radiated from the Messiah's face as he entered the domain of paradise. It was evening time. It was reunion time.

The first Adam did not see him coming because his eyes were consuming the first lady.

"Woman, I did it. I did it because our father gave us love, agape love that blinded me to your wrongdoing. I was the responsible person that should have said no, and it would have been over. But I didn't, so I bear the blame for it all. You were the one thing that stood out over all the other things that he gave me. I was and still am the one who should ask forgiveness.

"I should ask forgiveness for having blamed you instead of taking responsibility for my actions. But this moment, this instant, makes it all worth spending the time outside the Garden of Eden with you. I did not do what I was supposed to do. I shirked my duty as the one who was responsible, so now I ask you to forgive me!"

Adam and Eve were totally absorbed in each other and unaware of what was going on around them. Thus, they simultaneously jerked as the hand of the Messiah embraced them completely. Much to their surprise, everyone had heard every word that they spoke to each other and was beaming with joy and peace. They were forgiven. The Messiah, having heard the whole conversation, knew that he did not need to say any more to Adam about it.

"The father's will is done in this. I have gone down to Sheol and took away the power of Satan and the grave."

"Death no longer has dominion over him. For the death that he died, he died to sin once and for all; but the life that he lives, he lives to God. Likewise, you also reckon yourselves to be dead indeed to sin but alive to God in Christ Jesus our lord."[15]

"No longer do they have the power that they once wielded, for now I hold both keys. Death's influence has been nullified, and no longer has he the power of fear to back him against those who will believe that I'm the Messiah sent by the father to redeem them.

"Those who really believe will not fear Death's appearance in their lives because they know that he is there to take them to that place where we will all be in glory.

"This is the day that the Lord has made. We will rejoice and be glad in it!"[16]

David's words rang out for all of paradise to hear as he welcomed the Messiah to Abraham's bosom. "We have waited for you to come, Lord! We have waited!" His words became a chorus for all. "Paradise is alive in us as we are in it!"

John stepped through the crowd to embrace Christ, as did Adheres.

"We are so glad that you have come through unscathed by the environment of Hades, Messiah."

"Unscathed? That depends on your definition of the word, John! Do you think that you were unscathed by your sojourn on earth? I think not! Your head was cut off to satisfy the wanton desire of a sex-crazed man and his adulterous wife!

"No. I did not leave Hades unscathed. Otherwise, I would not have done what the father expected of me. It was for that purpose that I went there! I had to suffer as mortal man would. I had to suffer, bleed, and die to go there. And that was the hardest part of my task, something that no other person could have done.

"It is for that reason that I proposed to the father that I go, and now that it is over, I'm glad that I offered. It is done! Man's redemption is now paid in full!"

"Messiah, are you saying that you suffered there too?" John asked.

"More than I did on the cross or at the hands of Herod or Pontius Pilate's soldiers, John. More than both occasions had to offer!

"I had to suffer the same thing as any of you would have suffered had I not died on that tree! I had to feel the same things that you would have felt, every emotion, pain, joy, and sadness that you would have had to bear from birth to death!

"Only then could I understand what it meant when Lucifer won by beguiling Adam, my friend, and Eve. Without that experience, Death and Satan would have been able to make the argument that the price for your redemption was not enough."

Suddenly, it became quiet in paradise. No one thought that the Messiah had also suffered in Hades. No one expected to hear that.

"It was for that reason that I died in the first place, everyone! I took all your sins, from which you were temporarily reprieved, and bore them there. Then I too had to bear the pain of the fire as you would have, and many after you!

"I became flesh so that the experience of being man in the flesh would be real. My father could not leave anything to chance; otherwise, Satan would find a way to deny your freedom. If I did not go through that part of it, it would have been all for naught!

"I did not give up all my glory, which you will all see shortly, to not finish it. This is the only way that I could have taken away your sins completely. If not, when I left I would have brought those same sins with me."

Everyone in paradise flinched in repulsion. They had had a chance to see what sin really looked like when they watched him make his way through the gates of Hades. It was not a nice sight to behold. They knew then what he did for them. They knew then that had he not come, bled, and died, as Isaiah had foretold, they would be presently facing a different situation, one that they would not even want to give any thought to.

"That is some price!" Adam said, tears welling up in his eyes.

Eve, who stood by, was already crying because she knew and felt Christ's pain as he went through three nights and two days in Hades. She told no one, and most of all, she kept it from Adam who was bearing enough guilt as it was. Still, as she saw him walk down that path, she looked toward heaven and thanked the father for keeping his word to Satan and to her, the first woman.

"And I will put enmity between you and the woman, and between your seed and her seed. He will bruise your head, and you will bruise his heel."[17]

He had gone through the gate, but still she felt his pain and anguish. She knew that Hades was not the place to be.

Just then, another person stepped through the crowd to stand in the clearing around Christ. Jesus stood still and looked at the man intensely for a time before stepping forward, crying.

Everyone knew that this person, this man, was in paradise but had kept to himself most of the time. They couldn't understand why, until that moment. He had been the unknown factor in paradise until John came. John had spoken to him immediately upon showing, up and that raised the curiosity of everyone even more!

"Who is he?" Everyone would ask, but no one seemed to know. However, John did but would not divulge it. All he would say was, "In God's good time, it will be made known to you!"

"Father! Joseph! The father kept this from me! I looked all over Hades trying to find you! If I had found you there, I do not know what I would have done! Oh, it is good to see you, Father! Joseph!

"Mary's husband, yes!" Isaiah shouted! "You were the one who kept him safe while he grew into manhood. You were the one who ran with him into Egypt to escape Herod's anger and fear. You are his earthly father, Joseph! Why? Why did you not say anything?" Isaiah asked.

"Because . . . when she told me that she was pregnant with him, following our custom, I wanted to have her stoned! And that is something that I have never been proud of or unable to forgive myself," Joseph answered.

"Father!"

Jesus had always known Joseph's pain, particularly as he grew into manhood. He would catch his father unawares, looking at him with such pain and love. Jesus knew that Joseph had regretted even thinking of following the custom of the Israelites. Christ had already forgiven him.

But that is what makes humanity so unique—they cannot let go of guilt that easily. Once they know that they have done something wrong and admit it, it is only the beginning of a long burden.

"I know why the father loves them so. They do not easily forgive themselves. And Adam and Eve are prime examples of that," Jesus mused.

"Father Joseph, I had already forgiven you, from the time I exited my mother's womb. I saw the love that you showed for her and me, so I knew that you did not really want to hurt or harm either of us.

"This is why you are here and not there! You believed that I was the Messiah. You believed it and went about preparing me for it, although you did not let on about your belief. This you kept carefully hidden from me, and I suspect that the father assisted you in this.

"He is like that, you know. He is very funny sometimes. In fact, he has some of the greatest laughs just by looking at mankind and some of their antics. He knows that they—you—are special."

The environment changed as the scene between Christ and Joseph unfolded. First, there was sadness, followed by curiosity, then joy at recognition of the earthly father of Christ. Joseph was not a person of many words—that was obvious. So no one expected to hear much from him, but were they surprised!

The conversation between father and son took on a personal and intensely affectionate tone. Joseph asked numerous questions which Christ responded to, and vice versa. It was a wonderful experience to behold. Joseph opened up by explaining his love for Mary and Christ.

Joseph spoke of the intimacy he and Mary shared while she carried Jesus, and this received much attention from the residents of paradise. They were interested in knowing how Joseph coped with the situation, having to wait more than ten months before they could consummate their marriage vows.

It was a story that found a place in everyone's heart because of the touching ramifications of agape love. To wit, Christ responded that he too enjoyed the love that poured out from both of them.

"It was not a matter of physical love but a matter of God's love abiding within Mary," Joseph said. "Every time we touched each other, we knew that the precious gift within her must not be touched in any way by the temporal feelings that Satan tried to bring into play. Our responsibilities as parent overrode our responsibilities as husband and wife.

"You see, we quickly realized that this little bundle"—he touched Christ's shoulder—"was more important than both of us together. That was the impetus we needed in order to do what was right, righteous in the father's sight. Which was not to contaminate this awesome package that God had entrusted to us."

While the conversation went on, Christ mentally prepared himself for his next task; he was not yet finished with the process of redemption.

"We were not as important as the package itself, the Messiah. And so here we are!"

Salvation Comes to Paradise:
Night to Dawn of the Third Day

"This is a wonderful day, one that I have looked forward to ever since I spoke creation into existence. Finally, I'm now given the opportunity to set the captives free!"

It was a joyous occasion that was celebrated in heaven and in paradise.

"Mankind will soon know how these three nights and three days ended. They will know the importance of what transpired here in Hades and soon in paradise."

His thoughts continued to race ahead of him to that moment when he would finally give them the freedom that waited for them.

"They all thought that this was the ultimate, but they have no idea how much more awaits them."

John came forward and asked Christ, "How did you feel when you looked all over Hades and did not see or find Joseph?"

"I thought that he would not have hidden himself from me, knowing that I'm the Messiah! So when I left Hades, I left with a wounded heart, but for those who are there. But for him whom I did not see, I expected to find him here."

"Do you think that you made a mistake?"

"No! I did not see everyone in Hades because many of them were hiding from me, knowing that they had blown it. But Joseph would not have let me leave without saying hello and good-bye. It would have been a last minute thing but worth it under any circumstance.

"John, I have monitored Adheres' progress and yours over here, and I must say that you have performed wonderfully for the father. You have not disappointed him in any way. Well done, my good and faithful servant!"

"Coming from you, Messiah, that makes me know that I'm pleased to have served you, the father, and now the Holy Spirit! Yes, I'm glad that I have been worthy of this opportunity."

"Where is Adheres?"

"Oh, he is so excited at being here. I doubt that he has spent one second in any place since he got here. Oh, here he comes now!"

Adheres broke through the crowd with a spring and dance in his step, followed by David, the king of Israel. Adheres' momentum took him right into the arms of Christ, and there were tears on his face as he hugged the Messiah.

"Thank you. Thank you!" he squawked continuously. "Thank you for saving me from eternal damnation. I looked at Etchers over there, and I tell you it has been the most convicting thing I have ever witnessed. I have said, 'There but for the grace of Christ go I!' Thank you!"

David's approach was more serious, more purposeful.

"Messiah, I'm really thankful that the father has chosen my line, my throne, to be the one on which you will sit forever. I feel humbled seeing you for the first time."

"Oh, do you mean that you would have recognized me without my manifestation?"

"Only the Messiah could come in here, manifested or not, and command this attention. No other could and make the Bible true!"

"Well," said the Messiah, "I can see why the father said that you are a man after his own heart. I'm humbled to know that your kingdom is so established that I can rule over it forever.

"Moses! You stand so silent; why have you not spoken? Are you happy to see me?"

"Master, Messiah, I'm the happiest of all these people! However, I'm really disappointed that not many more of your chosen people are here. Have they fallen so far away from the father that they are spending eternity over in Hades instead of here? They, of all people, were whom I expected to see filling up this place. Why are they not present in abundance?"

"You know the answer better than any other person here, Moses. They were—and still are—the most stubborn people that the father has had to deal with!"

"Now I know why he chose us. Because if he did not, none of us would have been here! We would have ignored him completely, so he made us leaders instead of followers so that at least some of us—the remnants—would get here!"

"Well-spoken, Moses! Well-spoken. You see, the father will take those that are stiff-necked and place them in the yoke so that they may follow the path. In doing so, he has secured the people who learn to know him, to save some of them. It is the remnant that he is interested in because he knows that not all people will accept me! Satan has done a job of deception. Besides, we, the Godhead, knew before time, before the creation, that he would be successful in this area. But we also knew that there were those who would love God notwithstanding Satan's ploys. It is for this reason that I died before creation to circumvent this situation!"

"What do you mean that you died before creation?" This question came from Adam who was now seeing the full picture that was painted for his benefit.

"Yes, Adam, I was crucified before the beginning of creation in anticipation of this advent! You had a role to play, as did Eve.

"Eve!" Christ greeted. "You look wonderful! Oh, the father has blessed you with beauty and youth. You shine like a sun in full array. Yes, you are beautiful and every bit a mother to humanity."

Adam sensed that Jesus was purposely changing the subject and tried to bring it back, but the Messiah would have none of it.

"It is over! It is finished, Adam, and I'm here to consummate the deal for the remnant that the father would save. Know that and accept it, and know that you have done according to what was prescribed. The father loves you, Adam, and has never stopped so. All he asks of you is that you return that love—nothing more! Can you do that, Adam? Oh, I'm sure that you can. Otherwise, you would not be here in paradise today. So be happy! And, Adam, put away the guilt."

It was Eve's turn to question Christ, and he looked at her expecting the questions that brimmed her consciousness.

"Messiah, son, you are the one that the father told Satan about, coming from me, my seed?"

"Yes, I'm the one!"

"Then you died twice for mankind's salvation?"

"That is hard to explain to you at this time, but let us just say that I died once, although I also died before creation was spoken into existence."

"Hmm—"

"Eve, one day it will all become self-explanatory, but at this time you will not be able to fathom it! But in a very short time, you will."

Christ knew that she had more questions, but the answer he gave her would hold for now. She would understand when she reached heaven.

The air around them began to liven up as the idea of the Messiah being among them sank in. Still, they were unaware that this part of their happiness was to take on a new meaning, raising them to a higher level of consciousness. Some of them had been living in paradise for several thousands of years, enjoying all that it had to offer, and did not think that it could get any better than it was. But they were in for a surprise.

Christ had come to set the captives free, to lead them captive to this higher plateau of experience, provided that they accepted him as the Messiah. That part of his assignment seemed so easy; they were all people who had died expecting the Messiah to take away their sins forever. They were the ones who had made constant atonement for their sins using the blood of animals and birds as the father had asked. They were the ones who had wanted to be rejoined with the Creator, God, and followed his laws to the best of their ability. They were the remnants of the Old Testament. This was the reason why he took the keys of Hades and the grave from Satan. These people were still trapped in the grave—although for them, it was paradise. They could not go anywhere to be free without their graves being opened. The confines of their graves were the boundaries, the parameters, within which they had lived for thousands and hundreds of years.

But Christ now had the keys and was about to open them so that these wonderful souls could be set free. It was definitely a moment to look forward to, but they had no knowledge of it. It would be a surprise.

What Satan had not realized was that the keys to Hades and the grave were not physical keys; they were intangible. These were authorities that he had stolen from Adam and Eve when he seduced them into seeing things his way. The devil tricked Adam and Eve into saying and thinking certain things. When they did, they formally turned over the authority to speak things into reality. These were the keys, and among them was the command, the authority, to open the grave and Hades. Thus, Satan too had been tricked by Christ into saying that he had the authority. Immediately the keys had been transferred to Christ, giving him the authority to open the gates of Hades and the grave.

The gates of Hades opened one way—as did the grave—to let people in but not to let them out. Christ was able to walk in. He could not have left unless the devil had given up that authority. And so Christ used precision and time to his advantage. Three nights and three days it took, but it was worth it.

Satan had to be broken to the point where he felt that he had lost. There should be no vestige of hope left in him because that would have given him some clout or allowed him to be rebellious. A rebellious person does not just surrender; he has to surrender of his own free will. Satan was brought low to that point where he knew—not just felt—he had lost. And he did. He lost to Christ by condemning himself.

Christ used this newfound authority given to him by Satan to open the doors of Hades and leave. All the demons and other residents who looked on thought that he could not leave because they too had tried numerous times but failed. As a matter of fact, there was a multitude at the gate hoping that it would open for them, to the laughter of the gatekeeper. But they were not successful.

They had backed away as Christ came to the doors of Hades. They were snickering at what they thought would be a futile attempt. But to their amazement, the doors creaked and swung outward, opening for him to leave! The shouts that emanated from their throats were one of astonishment. They rushed to the gate, hoping to catch it open in time to escape. But the invisible barrier brought on by their sin would not allow them to go past the gates.

Satan had heard the news and was dumfounded. He really thought that he had the Messiah trapped with him for all eternity. However, the Messiah had flown his trap and left him to his fate.

"Now what? How did he get out?" Lucifer had shouted to the gatekeeper. That door opens for no one except you and me, so how did he get out?"

"I'm as perplexed as you, Master. Those doors simply swung outward and let him out!"

The occurrence caused Satan to recount all that happened while the Messiah was there, what led to all of it. After a long time of solitude, he jumped up and screamed, "I was tricked! I had the keys all the time and did not know it. I was tricked!"

Satan recalled how he had received the authority from Adam and Eve by tricking them. Now he knew that he had received a dose of his own medicine. It did not sit well with him.

"Where is David?" Jesus asked.

"Jesus, Lord, I'm here!" There was joy in David's voice. He knew now that God had forgiven him of the things that he did, particularly the situation with Bathsheba and Uriah. This thing had tormented him for so long. Even after he was given a reprieve by God, he still carried the guilt of what he had done.

"David, the father forgave you a long time ago when you acknowledged you were wrong and became penitent."

"Hmm, Teacher, you are the Christ, the son of the father. You are reading my mind."

"That is not all. I have been reading it all the way across the void in Hades. Absalom made a bad choice and did not ask for forgiveness. More important, he was an adult and, subsequently, responsible for his actions, as was Amnon. They did not take a page from your model to them. Otherwise, they would be over here and not there.

"Oh yes, they tried to hide from me, but their torment made it impossible to really hide. The pain was extensive. I should know because all the time I was there I was hurting too. Oh, I didn't let

Lucifer know that but I hurt, as he did. Now he is even hurting more because I brought every sin and placed them there to judge him. He will not soon forget those three days and nights with me in his domain.

"David, my father called you a man after his own heart, and it was not without reason. You admit your mistakes and reconcile them with him, especially after they are pointed out to you. But more than that, you love. You really love selflessly. This makes you stand out more than any other person on earth. I'm indeed privileged that the father chose your line for me to come through. It was a real honor, King David."

"Teacher, do not call me king. You are the king! I'm your servant."

"David, you were a king with a function that you carried out wonderfully. I too am a king, but with a function different from yours. Where is Bathsheba?"

"She is probably hiding behind someone because of what we did!"

"Bathsheba! You beautiful woman, come give me a hug! Bathsheba, stop hiding and come out here!"

A beautiful black woman stepped from behind Nathan, the prophet, and strode forward to embrace Jesus.

"You have given the father a wonderful ruler of the Israelites, young lady, so be proud. Because my father is very adept at taking, extracting, good out of evil. This hurts Satan more than anything else that has so far hurt him."

"Teacher, Messiah," Bathsheba said, "I salute you."

"The father has forgiven you of your sins, so forgive yourself also!"

The last function that Christ had to perform was ready. He called Noah, Abraham, Moses, Joshua, David, and John the Baptist to him. He gave them instructions; to wit, they too went out and called the twelve sons of Jacob. Abraham had three of the twelve sons, as did Moses, Joshua, David, and John the Baptist. These four parties were to divide the residents of paradise into equal numbers and line them up around the Messiah, encircling him. There was a hint of curiosity on their faces, but knowing who he was, they knew that he had a reason. Ezekiel was the first to understand what he was seeing and remembered:

> And I looked, and there in the firmament which was above the head of the cherubim, there appeared something like a sapphire stone, having the appearance of the likeness of a throne. Then he spoke to the man clothed with linen and said, "Go in among the wheels, under the cherub. Fill your hands with coals of fire from among the cherubim and scatter them over the city." And he went in as I watched . . . . The cherubim appeared to have the form of a man's hand under their wings, and when I looked, there were four wheels by the cherubim: one wheel by one cherub, and another wheel by another cherub. The wheels appeared to have the color of beryl stone. As for their appearance, all four looked alike as it was—a wheel in the middle of a wheel . . . . And their whole body with their back, their hands, their wings, and the wheels that the four had, were full of eyes all around. As for the wheels, they were called in my hearing, Wheel . . . . When the cherubim stood still, the wheels stood still, and when one was lifted up, the other lifted itself up, for the spirit of the living creature was in them. Then the glory of the Lord departed from the threshold of the temple and stood over the cherubim. And the cherubim lifted their wings and mounted up from the earth in my sight. When they went out, the wheels were beside them; and they stood at the door of the east gate of the Lord's house, and the glory of the God of Israel was above them. This is the living creature I saw under the God of Israel by the river Chebar, and I knew they were cherubim. Each one had four faces and each one, four wings, and the likeness of the hands of a man was under their wings. And the likeness of their faces was the same as the faces which I

had seen by the river Chebar, their appearance and their persons. They each went straight forward.[18]

Then Ezekiel said out loud so that everyone could hear, "This is a representation of what God had shown me when I was alive. He is recreating the power structure of the father's kingdom! Yes, that is it!"

Christ smiled and said to himself, I knew that he would have recognized it. "This is a tribute to my father; thus, this symbol shows that he has not forgotten those who loved him and served him in spirit and in truth."

The circle was formed to mimic the wheel of Ezekiel's experience. Abraham represented the patriarchal position from which Christ would redeem all who believed. It started with that circle, the wheel. Christ himself stood in the center of it all. Then what followed was the most beautiful and memorable event in the history of the paradise.

"Brethren, throughout your history, my father required that you make a blood sacrifice to him as a temporary atonement for your sins. This atonement lasted for one year only. But you did it because it was a symbol of the real thing that was to come—the Messiah, Christ. I'm that Messiah, whom you had looked for down through the ages. I'm here to rescue you from the grave in which you have been trapped."

"Did you say grave, Messiah? Are you saying that this paradise in which we have lived was the grave?" asked Jonah, who so far had kept quiet?

"Yes, Jonah, this is the grave for you, a resting place until I come and bring salvation from its grasp. I bring you salvation, and I bring you the ultimate blood sacrifice!"

Jacob, who stood by quietly, asked, "Where is the sacrifice?"

"I'm the sacrifice. I'm the one-time sacrifice that will suffice for all temporary sacrifices and do away with the need for any other from this moment on. I'm Christ, the Messiah, the perfect lamb slain to wash away every sin and sin stain. No longer will mankind have to kill an animal or dove to be temporarily free from the dominion of sin. I come to take their place and have done so."

All of paradise was suddenly very silent, and not a breath rustled the air. Nothing, no one, moved as if for fear that it was a dream that would evaporate. Time stood even more still than it had before because this was the moment of truth. The Messiah had come to perform the permanent gift of sacrifice for both those who resided in paradise and those who were still alive.

Jesus said, "I'm the way, the truth, and the life. No one comes to the father except through me. For that reason, I'm here to offer you freedom to enter into the father's presence. Will you accept it?"

The shout that followed resounded and ebbed and flowed and spilled over the void of paradise and into Hades. The joy of this proclamation was more than the residents could contain.

And so every resident of Hades heard it. They heard the questions and answers from the residents of paradise, and for a moment, their pain and anguish became secondary as they looked intensely at the far shores of paradise to see everyone jumping for joy. Salvation had come to paradise, and redemption was in the place. It stirred the very spirit and soul of everyone, including the residents on the far shores of Hades.

Satan knew what to expect now that he had given the authority back to Christ to free the residents of paradise. It troubled him more than the fact that he had lost to him. Satan's countenance hung like a wet rag, and all who saw him in that moment questioned themselves, remembering:

> And those who see you will gaze at you and consider you, saying, "Is this the man who made the earth tremble, who shook kingdoms, who made the world as a wilderness and destroyed its cities, who did not open the house of his prisoners?"[19]

Satan did not look like the almighty anymore because he had been consistently losing to the Messiah ever since the latter entered and left Hades. Some of them commented, "Is this the one whom I allowed to bring me to this end? What was I thinking?"

Meanwhile, the message was received with a warm and joyous heart by one and all in paradise. "Salvation is here," and that was all that mattered. The message descended on all of them like a blanket bringing warmth of love and everlasting life to them. At last, they can understand what it meant to be really free, to enjoy grace—unadulterated grace—and the joy that it brought. There were tears of joy spilling out of the orifice of their eyes. Christ, looking on, wondered what it would have been like if the people who were still alive were there to show that kind of love for him, the perfect lamb slain for them.

"Still, I do not have to fear because you, Father, have given me a wonderful group of men and women who will persevere to take my message of good news to the end of the earth for all times."

And so Jesus began the permanent cleansing of all the residents of paradise.

"To be able to leave here and go to a better place, the procedure is simple, and it is your choice. You must be cleansed by my blood, which becomes the atonement for your sins.

"The way you have been arranged is in accordance with what Ezekiel was exposed to during his life experience in talking to and meeting my father. Thus, each of you represents an addition to his body.

"Now, if you accept me as your Messiah, step forward, take your finger or hand, dip it into the blood that flows from my side, head, hands, or feet, and your cleansing will be complete."

Christ did not need to say anything more because everyone wanted to be first. However, they maintained order, as each one stepped to the fountain to be bathed in the blood of the perfect lamb and be free of contamination forever.

After they had completed the task that was placed before them, they automatically fell back to the positions that they were in previously, waiting. The sight was a wonder to behold, as everyone, after dipping into the blood, became transformed, as if bathed in translucent light. They glowed with a cleanness that made them whiter than the whitest snow of winter.

Each person of each tribe of every nation—Jew and Gentile—was cleansed by the blood of the Messiah, completing their transformation.

At the conclusion, paradise glowed with a luminance that reached the far shores of Hades. It was a sight to behold.

After everyone has gone back to their original line after changing, they continued with the formation of the wheel. Twelve spokes represented not only the twelve tribes of Israel but also the children of Abraham from every corner of the earth. In other words, they were automatically adopted into Abraham's family when they touched the blood of the Messiah. Finally, the wheel was in place. The sacrifice's blood had done what it was supposed to do, and all that was left was to take them home.

Christ declared, "Now it is time for us to go home to the father!"

"But, Messiah, we are home, are we not?" Adheres asked.

"No! We are not yet home. I have prepared a place for you that which would make this look like a stopping place. You must now go into the presence of the father where you really belong."

Again a shout went up, and the crescendo made every rock, every structure in Hades sway, as if in the throes of an earthquake. The Messiah's proclamation was well received, and so he looked toward heaven and the father to report.

"Father, it is done. Man's redemption is paid."

The entire population of Hades was in an uproar, and for the first time, Satan felt threatened by the residents. They now knew that he was not all that, and he had been instrumental in their downfall to this place. Worse, there was something going on over in paradise that had the attention of all Hades's residents. Satan kept mumbling to himself, "He has achieved his purpose. He has achieved his purpose."

"What did you say?"

"Huh? Oh, it is you, Death. I'm just recounting all that has transpired, and I have reached the conclusion that this Messiah outsmarted us and achieved his purpose. We have really lost, and more than we wanted to."

"But I have not lost anything," said Death.

"Yes, you have. Only that you have not yet known it, but it will come to you."

Death left the presence of Satan thinking on one hand that he did not like the way how the other demons and people were looking at Satan.

"I do not want to be near him at this moment because there may be some action to be taken by the demons and the people. I do not want to be included with him.

"Now what does he mean that I have lost also? That perturbs me, and I need some privacy to think about it. He seems too confident in that remark."

When Death had walked away from Satan, the first shout coming from the direction of paradise went up, to wit he remarked, "They seem to be quite happy over there. I wonder what happened. The Messiah must be stirring them up, and to think that this sort of behavior will go on for all eternity, within hearing distance of this place. Oh, that is going to be a nuisance.

"What does he mean that I lost something too? Hmm. Oh! I have to go. Someone is about to die, and I want to be there to see her reaction, which they historically do not enjoy!

"As a matter of fact, I daresay that none of them wants to face me! They are always scared out of their wits. Haha!"

"Oh! Hello, Death!"

"What? What is going on here? She is not afraid of me? And she is not committing suicide either? What gives?"

She saw the consternation in his eyes and responded, "Please, don't worry. I'm not afraid of your coming because I now go to a better place. In fact, I rather enjoy your being here to assist me in this accomplishment!"

"Is this? . . . No . . . it cannot be."

"Come on, Death. Do not stand there looking perplexed. It is time for me to meet my father and my redeemer, and you are holding me up. Come on, move it!"

"Oh, this is crazy. This woman is destined for paradise, I guess."

At the moment that he thought that, the second shout emanated from paradise. Salvation was complete. Death felt a voice speaking to him, the same voice that had previously spoken to him.

"Is it you, Messiah?"

"Yes, Death, this is one of those things that you have lost—the ability to scare those who now believe and confess me. Also, you will not bring her to paradise. Instead, you will take her up to heaven to my father because paradise is about to close. An angel will meet you and take her from you.

"You have also lost something else: in the future you will not be able to intimidate anymore those who confess me as their lord and savior!"

"I hear and obey you, Messiah."

"Brethren," Christ said, addressing the saved souls, "it is time to go! Please hold each other's hand as I lead you on your way to the father!"

The Messiah rose into the air above Abraham's bosom. As he rose, the first group of the wheel—Noah, Methuselah, Nimrod, Abraham, and those who had lived before Jacob—rose in a circle. The Messiah opened his hands and seemed to become a doorway filled with the most awesome light which bathed everyone.

The first group passed through the light and into nothingness, drifting upward. They were followed by the spokes of the wheel led by each leader of the twelve tribes of Israel.

The wheel formation ascended in perfect symmetry. Not one spoke was out of alignment as it rose into the rose-colored skies. Up, up, and up it rose. All eyes from Hades were fixed on it. It was a sight to behold. Abraham's bosom trailed upward, touching the heights of the heavens.

Hades looked on in sorrow, knowing what they had lost. What they had was nothing compared to what the residents of paradise had. Hades was fire and brimstone, pain, eternal worms ceaselessly tormenting their hosts, who also would not die but feel every sensation of pain, depression, and loss for all eternity.

Sorrow and joy filled the air that morning as the arc of paradise lights filled the skies for all of Hades to see. Paradise would be no more across the void. It would cease to exist as they knew it.

The longing to be on that side of the void will not haunt the Hades residents to want to be there because they will not see it anymore. But its memories would be constant reminders of what they had lost for all eternity. Dry sobs filled the whole panorama of Hades.

"There is no more void, no more hope, no more longing, nothing. Oh the pain, the loss!"

That was the most common cry to be heard that morning, which was beautiful for some and dreary for others. Hades would not be the same anymore, and neither would paradise. The third shout seemed to travel out of hearing as paradise also traveled out of sight.

Death, while transporting the dead woman, fought with that nagging feeling which he thought had gone away.

"There it is again! What have I not been able to remember? Hmm, now I feel that I desperately need to remember it, but what?" Then it dawned on him. "It was foretold! The Messiah would come and lead the captives free! And there was nothing that anyone in Hades could do to stop it. Moreover, he will strip the grave of its powers, take away some of mine, and reduce the devil's ranking.

"Oh me! It has all happened as it was foretold! And soon he will return. This time he will judge the devil and myself and put us into Tartarus with other demons, the false prophets, the anti-Christ, and those who have been the worst of all mankind. Too late, it is all falling into place, and I can do nothing about it."

The cavalcade from paradise ascended into the heavens, just as it was formed by Christ. The wheel remained intact, with no one breaking the ranks to get there faster. All the angels of heaven had been on the lookout for this wondrous spectacle. They had begun singing before the wheel appeared. Their song expressed what had transpired from the moment of Christ's death until it was announced that they were on their way. They sang the song of joy as they sighted the wheel spinning and coming toward heaven. Two songs eventually met and blended into one: that of the angels and that of the humans. They sang a song of praise. Redemption's price had been paid. The grave had given up the dead.

"Wait. Messiah, are you not going with us?"

"I will be along shortly. I still have some unfinished business waiting for me to be accomplished on earth. However, the father is waiting for you with open arms. Abraham will present you to the father. Now rise up and be on your way!"

The third roar filled the air as all of paradise began rising toward heaven. This third shout brought the entire Hades to the borders to see a most magnificent sight.

> He who has an ear let him hear what the Spirit says to the churches. To him who overcomes, I will give to eat from the tree of life, which is in the midst of the paradise of God.[20]

Endnotes

1. The New King James Bible: Ever-increasing Faith Study Bible, Matthew 19:26, Thomas Nelson, Inc., 1994.
2. Ibid., Luke 23:39.
3. Ibid., Luke 23:40-41.
4. Ibid., Luke 23:42.
5. Ibid., Luke 23:43.
6. Ibid., Matthew 16:26-27.
7. Ibid., 2 Peter 3:9.
8. Ibid., Matthew 27:54.
9. Ibid., John 10:31.
10. Ibid., John 14:6.
11. Ibid., Luke 23:40-41.
12. Ibid., Luke 23:39-43.
13. Ibid., Matthew 16:26.
14. Ibid., Jude 6-7.
15. Ibid., Romans 6:9-11.
16. Ibid., Psalms 118:24.
17. Ibid., Genesis 3:15.
18. Ibid., Ezekiel 10.
19. Ibid., Isaiah 14:16-17.
20. Ibid., Revelations 2:7.

Edwards Brothers Malloy
Thorofare, NJ USA
April 16, 2013